Killing Me Softly

Also by John Leslie

Blood on the Keys
Bounty Hunter Blues
Killer in Paradise
Damaged Goods
Havana Hustle

Killing Me Softly

A Gideon Lowry Mystery

John Leslie

POCKET BOOKS
New York London Toronto Sydney Tokyo Singapore

This book is a work of fiction. Names, characters, places, and incidents are either products of the author's imagination or are used fictitiously. Any resemblance to actual events or locales or persons, living or dead, is entirely coincidental.

POCKET BOOKS, a division of Simon & Schuster Inc., 1230 Avenue of the Americas, New York, NY 10020

Library of Congress Cataloging-in-Publication Data

Leslie, John, 1944–
Killing me softly / John Leslie.
p. cm.
ISBN 0-671-86420-3
I. Title.
PS3562.E8174K55 1994
813'.54—dc20 93-26083
CIP

First Pocket Books hardcover printing May 1994

10 9 8 7 6 5 4 3 2 1

Printed in the U.S.A.

John Melville Leslie
(1922–1957)

Acknowledgment

To Bill Grose for a decade of
sound advice and encouragement.

1

No flats . . . . Hitched and hiked and grifted, too, from Maine to Albuquerque. Fingers gliding across the cool keys. *Bah da da da dah, da da da da duh.* Huh? Image of Sinatra in a slouch hat, tie askew, cigarette dangling from the corner of his mouth. *Pal Joey.* Another era. The phrasing, get the phrasing right. And never bother with people I hate. An unnatural A-flat coming up. There. That's why the lady is a tramp.

Over the top of the baby grand, I saw a woman come in, sit at the bar. The same one who'd been in here last night. Dressed in white. A long, full-length gown, more like a robe really, with a scarf or something covering her head. Thin. Like an apparition. Or maybe she'd been cloistered all her life.

Behind the bar, Ronnie served her a cocktail in a tall glass, which the woman in white cradled in both hands.

I segued into "Summertime." Allegretto semplice. C- and F-sharp. In Key West the livin' is supposed to be easy. In my head, hearing Mahalia Jackson. Probably not half a dozen people in here who would remember Mahalia Jackson. Michael Jackson? Oh, man, how times do change.

On the acoustic guitar behind me, Harry beat out the rhythm.

I closed out the set with "Nice Work If You Can Get It" and stood up from the piano to scattered applause. This wasn't concert work, just background; loosen them up before they went off into the Key West night. Mellow fellows. Golden oldies.

"Next set we'll capture them with Cole Porter," I told Harry.

Harry was young but a fine musician. We'd played together for a couple years now. He nodded and headed out, probably to fill his nose with the demon powder. I went to the men's room, took a long leak, and came back to the bar.

Ronnie had my usual ready. Barbancourt rum over ice with just a splash of soda to drag it out. "It's on the nun," Ronnie said, tossing her beautiful head in the direction of the woman in white.

Ronnie was this season's femme fatale behind the bar. Young, beautiful, promise-them-anything as long as they stayed at the trough. She'd be here a season, maybe two, then like so many others before her, be gone.

I often wondered what it was that drew these young women to Key West, but more I wondered where they went from here. North, I suppose, back to some city where they could find someone to have and to hold. This was just a party town. You burned bright here for a time, but sizzled faster. Some basic instinct for survival must get them out before they saw themselves fading into the woman in white with whom I touched glasses.

"Mr. Lowry?"

"Gideon," I said. *Gideon Lowry at the piano.* It was on the billboard by the elevator on the ground floor of the hotel.

"Virginia." Not Ginger, or Ginny. And carefully enunciated as if she might have to work at it. I noticed a slight tremor in her hand, which wasn't offered.

Up close her face was old, but seamless. Not old, ageless. I'm fifty-seven myself, a relic in Key West. But it's my town. Apart from a couple years in Korea, I've spent my life here.

"Those old songs are awfully sentimental, aren't they?" Virginia said.

"Pure schmaltz," I said.

"But addictive."

"Like so many things that aren't good for you."

Virginia studied her drink as if I'd rebuked her. That wasn't intended. I have my own problems in that area. I don't know why people are inclined to buy musicians drinks. It's unnecessary because when we work, they're on the house. More lost souls looking for comfort. Or condolence.

"Did you grow up here?" Virginia asked. "I don't remember you."

"You're from here?"

Virginia shook her head. "My parents moved here when my sister and I were in school. I graduated from Key West High. Class of '55."

A couple of years after I had. "What's your last name?"

"Murphy."

"I was in Korea when you graduated."

She nodded. A forgotten war and nearly half a century later our troops were still sitting over there huddled along the thirty-eighth parallel.

"My sister, Lila, was a year older than me. She graduated in '54."

Lila Murphy. It rang a bell but I couldn't place her. Like so many names and faces that swept in and out of this place from year to year.

"You aren't living here now, I take it."

Virginia lifted her glass and drank. Set it down for Ronnie to refill. "Savannah. I was born there."

I'd driven through there once, and once was enough.

The smell that hung over the area from the paper mills was something you didn't forget.

"My father was a lawyer," Virginia said. "Or more accurately, a fisherman who practiced law. That's why we moved here. Now they're all dead." She looked away.

I sipped my drink. I was trying to pace myself. There were still a couple hours to go. Harry was back on the stand, quietly strumming chords. He seemed okay.

"What about your family?" Virginia asked. "Are they still here?"

"Mostly dead. Or living somewhere else."

I looked out the bank of windows behind the bar where a few boats, shapeless in the dark, were recognizable merely by their red or green navigational light, like a garish Cyclops. "Thanks for the drink," I said. This conversation had the prospect of turning maudlin. "I've got to get back to work."

Virginia didn't seem to hear. "Lila's dead, too."

"I'm sorry."

"You must have been in Korea when she was killed. I'd like to talk to you about it."

I was retreating to the stage. "Anytime."

I set my drink on some sheet music stacked on the piano and sat down.

" 'It's All Right With Me.' E-flat," I told Harry. *Ba ba bah.* Talk about the wrong time and the wrong place.

I should have dedicated it to Virginia Murphy. Somehow I knew I hadn't seen the last of her.

2

In 1956 when I returned from Korea, Key West was much the same as it had been when I left in '54. Today of course it's only a distant memory of that time. The neighborhoods are still familiar, and the sea, but what has changed are the people and the fabric of the city. Gone for the most part are those gritty Conch faces, hidden now behind six-foot fences, or buried along with my parents and cousins in the concrete tombs stacked one on top of the other in the city cemetery.

I miss them. A few still remain, of course, those who haven't fled before the carpetbaggers and reconstructionists of the seventies.

These young, bland faces of today, with their sunburns and peeling noses, have turned this town into any other sun-drenched coastal outcropping with its appeal to the masses. Fast food. Fast life. And slow death.

I'm not complaining. There's not enough fish in the sea anymore to support that industry, so stocking the pond with tourists is a matter of survival I suppose, but I miss the old people and the old ways. Call it nostalgia, but personally I think things were better back then.

After Korea I should have gone back to school, gotten into college somewhere, and gotten out of here. But I was lulled. The truth is I had damned little ambition other than what I could get from a bottle.

I fished for a couple of years but without much success since I'm prone to seasickness. Worked as a fireman for a while and spent several years as a cop with Key West's finest. Both jobs that were controlled by the city, and Conchs for many decades. B.C. Before the carpetbaggers. Weekends I played piano for a couple of different bands around town, playing weddings, Elks' parties, and a club or two.

In the sixties I went into business for myself, opening a detective agency on Duval Street. If all this sounds like kids' stuff, that's because it is. Cops, firemen, fishermen. Like a lot of people in Key West, I guess I never grew up.

Three wives would probably agree with that.

The Lowry detective agency is still listed in the phone book, and I'm still on Duval Street, although several blocks up from where I originally started. In a small Conch house that's withstood the elements and efforts by any number of chichi boutique owners, or whatever they call themselves these days, to buy me out and put in something that would look like everything else on Duval.

I like the street. There's something comforting about having an ocean and a gulf at either end of it, knowing the buck stops here, as one of our many famous winter residents once said.

I live alone in the back in a couple of rooms with the large front room my office. A desk, a phone, some filing cabinets. A few pictures and one large tomcat who likes to sleep in one of the desk drawers I leave open for him.

A lot of my work is for the state attorney's office. I seek people out for depositions and deliver subpoenas. Hunt for witnesses to crimes. And sometimes I get a private call to spy on a wayward spouse, but not much of that anymore. Today you don't need an excuse to dump somebody.

Those same three wives will attest to that, too. That

kind of responsibility never suited me and I've given up pretending otherwise.

Weekends I still manage to keep a gig going in one of the clubs around town. Usually waking up on Monday morning with a hangover. There's always a bottle in the office and a few in the back, but I do most of my drinking now when I play. So far so good. One weekend at a time is my motto.

This Monday I slept in. At eight I got up and fed Tom, took a couple of aspirin, unplugged the phone, then went back to bed. I wasn't expected anywhere and had no place I wanted to be. I dreamed of pirates.

At ten I got up and showered, got a Cuban coffee from the *grocería* next door, and began to face the day. Looking out the uncurtained window to the back of a parking lot, deserted and unused except for my own car, which I seldom used.

The sun was shining, signaling another glorious day in paradise. Another day to promote to the tourists. Running my hand over the stubble of gray hair on my head, I decided to get a haircut. One of the habits acquired from two years in the U.S. Marine Corps was a fondness for short hair. Regrettably perhaps it was the only habit left over from those years.

Wearing a pair of khaki pants and a T-shirt, I stepped out into the front office to see if there was any mail, which these days consisted mostly of bills and circulars. And too damned few checks. From the floor I picked up a handful of each that had been pushed through the slot in the door. Then I made the mistake of opening the dusty venetian blinds that cover the front windows.

A guy was dusting off the used cars on the lot across Duval Street.

And Virginia Murphy was sitting in the swing on my

front porch, wearing the same habit she'd had on last night. She looked frail, much more so than she had when I last saw her sometime in the early hours before closing. Her face now was pale and sweaty.

I opened the door, invited her in, then made the mistake, after seeing her appearance, of offering her a drink.

3

With the bottle of Barbancourt and two cups of *café con leche* on the desk, I sat down in the swivel chair facing Virginia Murphy. She seemed engulfed in the large wicker chair I'd picked up a long time ago at some forgotten yard sale.

Tom must have got the scent of female because he left his bed in the desk drawer and sauntered around to Virginia, jumping into her lap. She stroked him with her free hand, the one that wasn't clutched around the glass. Tom's motor went into overdrive. He has a thing for women, probably because I don't particularly like cats and don't encourage this kind of behavior. I took him in a couple years ago when I found him lying under the step out in back, the victim of some turf war in the neighborhood.

I'm a sucker for victims.

When I finished the last set at the Club, sometime around two A.M., quite a crowd had gathered in the bar, and after a nightcap with Harry, the one that I didn't need, I skipped out and was in bed by three. From the looks of Virginia she hadn't been quite so lucky.

"You didn't spend the night in that swing, did you?" I asked.

She shook her head almost as if she were reluctant to speak for fear of the mess she might make of it. A feeling I'd known myself. I poured her a second shot and added one to my coffee. Already breaking the ground rules. It was only eleven o'clock in the morning. The weekend was over.

I tried to remember some of our conversation of the night before. There was something about her sister, whose name wouldn't come to me, which must have been the reason she was seeking me out. The sister was dead. And we'd all gone to Key West High School forty long years ago.

"Where are you staying?" I thought I'd better know just in case she completely wigged out on me.

"A boardinghouse on Smith Lane."

There were a couple. I gazed at Virginia. Something clicked. "Big Betty's?"

Virginia nodded.

A lezzie hangout. At one time, in the forties, it had been one of several brothels that had flourished in Key West, catering to the military.

Virginia took a drink. Her skin was pale, the flesh stretched taut against the delicate bones of her face, a face without wrinkles. She wasn't pretty exactly, but there was something beatific about her, childlike, as though she'd been frozen in time.

"How long have you been here?"

"Three days."

"Alone?"

She nodded again.

"You came here to see me?"

"Someone. I asked around. Your name was mentioned."

Mentioned. Not recommended.

"About your sister?"

Again she nodded, finished her drink, and eyed the bottle. I poured her another shot.

"You want to tell me about her?"

Virginia hesitated before taking the plunge, her eyes watery as a swampy wetland in the dry season.

"Lila"—she breathed the name as though giving life to it. I tried to let her find her own pace—"was killed in 1955."

One of the two years I was in Korea.

"Only nineteen years old. Her body wasn't discovered until a week later."

"Where was she found?"

Virginia put a hand to her eyes. It was hard to know if she was overcome by emotion or the rum. "Some weeds up the Keys."

Lila Murphy. I leaned back in the chair, tried to cast my mind back through all the dust and cobbled webs of time; through the hazy dimness of too much booze and the nearsightedness of an uncertain present.

I got out of the Corps in August of '56 and came back to the sultry dampness of a Key West summer. I remembered those big puffy clouds low down, stretching in a line over the land along the Keys the way they did in summer, full of moisture. And despite the clammy atmosphere, how glad I was to be home.

I sweated out the rest of the summer with my mother in the big house on William Street where my brother and I had grown up. I drank a lot, went out with the old gang, staying up until three or four o'clock in the morning, then sleeping till noon. Trying to get back in the swing of things, like I was in high school again, but it wasn't the same. I didn't feel right; things were out of joint.

Carl, my brother, five years older than I, was an aide to Senator John T. Bayard, Monroe County's state senator, living in Tallahassee then. Or maybe Carl had been elected to the legislature, his first elective office. I couldn't remember. Carl had gotten all the ambition in our family. He later succeeded John T., who retired sometime in the seventies from the Senate, where Carl has been ever since.

When I came home from Korea, my father was retired from City Electric and was operating a charter fishing boat; he spent a lot of time on the water.

Mother didn't criticize me, just let me find my way. I was a Conch boy after all and Conch boys had strong family connections. Islanders, too, I think are like that. Which never explained this remoteness that came over me later in life.

My friends and I hung out at the Garden of Palms. I remember the colorful lanterns hanging from the ceiling of the outdoor bar. I caught up on all the local gossip and it must have been there at the bar that I heard about Lila Murphy. I didn't know her, or don't remember knowing her.

There wasn't a lot of murder in Key West back then, and still isn't, so it would have been something to talk about many months after it had happened.

By Christmas I had taken my first job with the fire department, rented my own place, and was going out with the woman who would become the first Mrs. Gideon Lowry.

I poured Virginia yet another shot and added a touch to my cold coffee. "Your family didn't stay here?"

"We moved back to Savannah six months after Lila was found."

"And this is your first time in Key West since then?"

"Yes."

I didn't have to ask if it was hard for her, nor why she was here. I could see it in her eyes, those watery lenses that fixed on me. She wanted to unravel the mystery, solve a crime, put finis to something that had left her face with this haunted, empty look.

And she wanted me to do it.

After fixing her some soup, I called a cab and bundled Virginia Murphy into the back, giving the driver a twenty-dollar bill for a five-dollar ride and telling him to take her to Big Betty's and make sure she got to her room without problems and without having to depend on the kindness of strangers. A quote from another famous resident of ours. I introduced Virginia to the cabdriver to make sure he got my meaning.

It was two o'clock when I got on my bicycle with its balloon tires and the big wire basket where I carried a tire pump for emergencies. A very old-time Conch habit. Something you don't see much anymore.

I pedaled over to the public library, the pink building on Fleming Street, parked at the bike rack out front, and locked up.

I found Mary Russell in the back room of the archives. The arc. What Mary doesn't know about Key West history isn't worth knowing. She was at her desk going through some old photographs that had just come in.

Mary barked a greeting in her raspy voice. She was asthmatic, not helped by a lifetime of smoking. Although a few years older than I am, I remember Mary, too, from the Garden of Palms, when she lit up the place with her wit and intelligence.

"Lila Murphy," I said.

"What about her? She's dead." Mary didn't miss a beat turning the photos.

"You remember her?"

"Who could forget those looks?"

"You got a picture of her?"

"Probably, someplace."

"And the newspaper files?"

"On fiche."

"I'd like to take a look," I said.

Mary sighed and stood up, walking slowly around the desk to the files where the microfiche were kept. She went straight to the drawer and pulled out the box that contained a roll of film of the *Key West Citizen* for 1955.

"I don't remember the month but I think it was in the spring. You want me to put it on the machine for you?" Mary asked.

"I think I can manage it."

Mary looked at my unshaven face, the bloodshot eyes, and smiled. It seemed to me the smile might have been tinged with regret; perhaps for the toll that our dissolute lives had taken.

The sketchy details of the disappearance of Lila Murphy were in the April 17, 1955, *Citizen*. Two nights earlier she had attended a dance at the local Elks club on Duval Street. She had danced with several local men and had been seen at the bar talking with a man none of the locals knew. No one remembered seeing her leave the party. The article described her as beautiful and popular, gave her parents' name, and her address.

I photocopied that story and the follow-up stories that appeared two or three times over the next several days. There were quotes from the sheriff, whose office was investigating the disappearance. They were following up on several leads according to Sheriff Paine.

Frank Paine was now dead. Had been dead for at least a decade if memory served. Which it often didn't.

In successive articles those leads were never mentioned again and Paine was seldom quoted.

A week after Lila's disappearance her body was discovered by some kids playing in the weeds up the Keys in Sugarloaf not far from the bat tower out behind where the Sugarloaf Lodge is today.

Sheriff Frank Paine would not say whether foul play was suspected in the death of Lila Murphy.

As I was copying this story, Mary came in and handed me a photo of Lila. A grainy black-and-white five-by-seven showing a brunette, about five feet seven, 125 pounds, according to the descriptions I'd just read. She was pretty. Smiling, winsome, I thought.

"Not bad," I said.

"Surprised you didn't make a play for her in high school. Or did you?" Mary asked.

I shook my head. "Not my type." I was surprised, however, that I didn't remember her and assumed that it was because she was an outsider, new in school, and as a Conch I was conditioned to being leery of outsiders. By the time Lila was out of school and apparently bewitching my peers, I was, of course, in Korea. "What was her type?"

"She didn't discriminate. In my opinion she was too young for most of the men that she went after. But that didn't stop her, or them."

"Any names come to mind?"

"All of them. Lila turned all their heads. They were like dogs in heat whenever she was around."

"Sounds like she might have trampled on some of your ground."

"I would have scratched her eyeballs out," Mary said, grinning.

Mary was a spinster, never having married, and it was not inconceivable that she would have been envious of someone with Lila's looks.

I put away the fiche and asked Mary if I could hang on to the photo for a while.

"What for?"

I didn't really know. I just wanted it, I told her.

Mary waved her hand to dismiss me and dug into the box of photos on her desk.

I put the five-by-seven of Lila in my pocket, went out to my bike, and rode over to Peggy Maloney's. Formerly Peggy Lowry, the first Mrs. Gideon Lowry.

Peggy Baker Lowry Maloney. Like many Conch women Peggy had grown a little thick in the ankles, but she still looked good for a woman at the end of her sixth decade. We all had something to show for this life in the sun. Peggy had a husband, a grown son, and a daughter who was in her last year of high school. Key West High. The same place I'd met Peggy. It didn't seem possible that so many years had gone by, and here we were looking at each other across her kitchen table over a cup of coffee like it was yesterday.

A couple times a month I would stop by for coffee and gossip. Peggy was the only one of the exes who regarded me with anything more than disdain.

I like to think that it was the issue of kids that separated us, but I know that in all likelihood I wasn't cut out to be a husband. Not for seven days a week, fifty-two a year anyway.

Peggy wanted kids. I didn't. After seven years of marriage she got tired of trying to change my mind and moved on to Jake Maloney. Jake filled the bill, so to speak. And Peggy and I remained friends.

"Rough night?" Peggy asked, giving me the once-over.

"I didn't pace myself."

Peggy had given up booze years ago. She once told me that she and Jake had smoked a lot of marijuana before the kids got into high school, then quit in order not to have conflicting attitudes at a sensitive time for them. Peggy had never confided any major family problems so I suppose she felt a kind of achievement, having succeeded in what she set out to do.

"You play last night?"

I nodded. When we were married, I'd played several nights a week, not just weekends, and those late nights away had been a source of contention between us. Inevitably, there'd been accusations of other women; toward the end of our time together, accusations not altogether unjustified. In fact, I met the woman who would become the second Mrs. Lowry at a club I was playing.

"So, Bud, how's life treating you?"

I shrugged. For a reason I'd forgotten Peggy had always called me Bud, a nickname that had caught on. Every so often on these visits she found it necessary to inquire if I was happy or how life was treating me. I never had an answer for either question. Happy? I don't know. Some days I was, some not. But I knew Peggy wasn't asking about one day in the life of Gideon Lowry.

"The name Lila Murphy mean anything to you?" I asked Peggy.

She thought about it, biting her lip in a familiar way, then shook her head. "Who is she?"

I took the photo of Lila from my pocket and handed it to Peggy.

"It's an old picture. Am I supposed to know her?"

"She was in high school a year or two behind us. Her body was found up in Sugarloaf around the bat tower. In 1955."

"Oh, I remember. Yeah, Lila Murphy. I'd forgotten her name. And her face." Peggy looked at the photo more closely. "My God, where'd you get this?"

"Mary Russell at the library."

Peggy shook her head. "Lila Murphy. I never really knew her. But she was something. She wasn't a local. And she was beautiful. Everyone was really jealous."

"You remember anything else about her?"

"Not really. She ran with a fast crowd, hung around adults, going to all the party dances at the Elks and the Jaycees."

"She hang out with anyone special?"

"Oh, God, Bud. I can't remember something like that. You're the one with the good memory."

Ravaged by time and booze, though I didn't say so to Peggy. "I was in Korea."

"That's right. Well, I don't know. Why are you interested in her after all these years?"

"They never found out what happened to her."

"It was a long time ago."

"I know. Her sister Virginia's in town. She's hired me to dig it all up."

"That's sad. What's she like?"

"Kind of a mousy type. Probably was always in Lila's shadow. And still is." I took a sip of coffee. "How's Jake and Barbara?"

"They're fine."

I finished my coffee and stood up. There really wasn't anything else to talk about. Ten minutes once or twice a month to see what I'd missed. Or escaped. Keeping a connection alive.

"Be careful," Peggy said as I was leaving. I wasn't sure why she said it, but it sounded like a warning.

"Always," I said.

On my way to the barbershop I biked past the homestead on William Street. Took a look at it as I always do when I pass there. The house was two-story, with a big front porch and a balcony on the second floor. There was a royal poinciana tree in the front yard whose fiery flowers shed each summer covering the sidewalk. It had been my job to sweep them up.

The house was a guesthouse now, catering to a male-only clientele. With its perfectly coiffed grounds and the rows of flowerbeds it seemed remote. An unlikely place to grow up, to be a kid in, but in the 1940s it had been different. And so was I.

6

Many of the old turn-of-the-century houses had been built by ships' carpenters from the Bahamas. Their basic frames could withstand storm-force winds, but they were little more than shells, designed more for comfort from the sultry tropical weather than for any aesthetic appeal. Other than a little gingerbread added to the porch railings and balustrades, the dwellings were austere. As austere as the economy in an island city a hundred and fifty miles from anywhere. For economic reasons we mostly just painted the fronts of our houses, leaving the sides and rear to weather.

These dwellings had little value. As they settled on their cinder-block foundations, they lost their true—floors sloped, walls were no longer square. The old tin roofs began to leak, and you could live in the family manse for next to nothing, but forget about it if you wanted to sell. They had no value because no one wanted these albatrosses. Until the carpetbaggers began coming.

They bought our homes cheap in the late sixties and early seventies, scraping and painting, knocking out walls, putting swimming pools in backyards, turning them into winter homes and guesthouses for the rich.

My brother, Carl, and I sold the house on William Street in 1978, a year after Mom died. And just before the big boom. We split a little under a hundred grand. By that time Carl was a senior senator, his ambition fully realized, and spent most of his time in Tallahassee. He has an office here in Key West and a small apartment he keeps for his infrequent visits back to his Monroe County constituents. He would have been happy if I'd wanted to keep the family home, but it was too big for one person to keep up and I wasn't going to be marrying again anytime soon.

My portion of the money from that sale went to buy the place I'm in now on Duval Street.

All happy families are alike, ours was unhappy in its own way, to paraphrase another famous writer—one of the few who didn't come to Key West. My father, William "Billy" Lowry III, was fourth-generation Conch. Captain Billy. His boat, the *Low Blow,* had been one of the early charter boats of the Key West deep-sea fishing fleet back in the fifties when that industry was budding.

He died in 1958 before the fleet grew to the size it is today with those half-million-dollar boats lined up along the south side of Garrison Bight, all those plastic fish strung up on blocks behind them, competing for clients.

Most of his life my father had been a lineman for City Electric. He retired in 1950 and went fishing, following his true love. And I've got no doubt that encompassed his wife, my mother. Phyllis was a freshwater Conch. She wasn't born in Key West, but having spent most of her life here she was given the nod by the local bubbas.

I suspect Phyllis would have liked to have gotten out of Key West, but by the time the Captain died her life here was too entrenched, and she had nowhere else to go. She came to Key West in the late twenties on her own at a time when most women didn't travel alone. Phyllis was something of a rebel for those days. She'd even gone to college in South Carolina, one of those colleges for women where she learned the social graces, and Latin. She came to Key West with some pretensions, which wasn't the greatest of resources for surviving here, then or now, but there were always books in the house. And music. The Captain was probably initially impressed with my mother's sophistication, but as the years went by I think he found it tedious.

While Carl and I were growing up, they fought a lot and there would be days when my father was never around. I don't know where he went. Fishing perhaps. Or to stay with the many relatives around the island; or he may even have shacked up with another woman for all I know.

In December 1957, my father was told he had cancer. Leukemia. He was sixty-one years old. Three months later he went down to the dock to his boat early one morning, sat in the wheelhouse, and shot himself in the head with the handgun he kept on board for killing sharks.

Another charter captain found Billy's body and reported it to the police, where I'd recently gone to work. I was on duty that morning and was one of the first to arrive at the *Low Blow.* There was a note so there was no question of what had happened.

I remember how I felt when I touched my father's dead body, picked him up and carried him off the boat to the dock where there was a waiting ambulance. Afraid my mother might show up there, I cleaned the boat to spare her any gruesomeness, then went to the house and was the first to break the news to her. She cried, but her face was twisted into some sort of rictus, so that it looked as if she were also laughing, reminding me of those theater masks depicting tragedy and comedy.

By the time Phyllis died, twenty years later, most of the Lowry family had moved on, leaving Key West for Ocala and Georgia, a couple of the places where Conchs had begun settling to escape the taxes and resort prices, and I was like a stranger in the town where I'd grown up.

At home I fed Tom his second meal of the day, then called Carl in Tallahassee, leaving a message on his answering machine. Afterward, I went to the Cuban restaurant that was a block away and got an early dinner. *Pollo asado.* Black beans, yellow rice, and warm Cuban bread lathered with butter. I ate alone, joking with Yolanda, the Cuban waitress.

My relationship with Carl has mellowed over the years, although six months can go by when we don't communicate. Carl is a politician and everything about him speaks of politics. If anything, I'm apolitical. Although I've had my differences with Carl. Politicians are opportunists, and Carl can change clothes with the best of them.

I finished my meal and walked back home. It was a beautiful May evening, the scent of frangipani and jasmine in the air, the temperature fading with the sunset. It left me feeling unaccountably sad. I walked into my office, and the first thing I saw was the bottle of rum on my desk, left there from Virginia Murphy's visit. More than half-empty.

I sat down, put my feet up, looked at the bottle for a while, then poured a slug of rum into the empty coffee cup I'd left there. An hour later it was totally dark, the bottle was empty, and I sat staring out the window at the passing parade, my thoughts buzzing around the room like a trapped fly.

"Be careful," Peggy had said. Dear Peggy. So boring in her domestic needs but, among her attributes, was the nonignorable fact that she was a great lay. Thinking back on that, I hoped I hadn't arrived at an age when sex was going to become a matter of reminiscence.

I stood up, knocked the bottle over as I went to close the slatted blinds. Then, walking to my apartment in back, I flipped on lights and went into the bathroom where I tried to shave. Nicked myself a couple of times and came out wearing tabs of toilet paper on my face to stem the bleeding.

"Dah, da da da dah. Dah da dah." The old upright

was in the bedroom, its keys sticky, sheet music piled on top of it. I sat down on the swivel stool and tried to pick out the melody. Who was it, Aretha Franklin? "Killing Me Softly." With your smile. With her smile.

The phone rang. Plunking away, I let it blend in with the out-of-tune piano before going to the kitchen and picking up the extension on the fourth ring.

Carl. "Bud," he said. He'd gotten that from Peggy. "What's up?"

"Making the family connection." My diction may have slipped a little on *connection*.

"You okay? You drinking?"

Yeah, I'm drinking. What else makes any sense when you think about it? "I'm fine," I said.

We were all so damned remote. Carl just disappeared into that Tallahassee life. I tried to remember where he was when the Captain died. He came for the funeral, which was kind of a big production. The black jazz band escorting Captain Billy into the cemetery. Somewhere there were some old photos of that. Mary Russell probably had them. Me in a suit standing between Peggy and Phyllis. Carl on the other side of Phyllis at the crypt.

Carl wasn't married, had never married. I don't think I ever saw him out with a woman. Because of illness during his youth, Carl had never been robust, which may have accounted, at least partially, for the lack of attention he received from girls. Over the years, I'd wondered if he might be gay, but we never discussed his personal life. Now, I believe he just wasn't sexual. Some people marry the church; Carl married politics. God, he was sixty-two now, and his life had been spent in politics in Tallahassee.

"You ever think of retiring?" I asked. I could picture him sitting ramrod straight in his apartment, silver-haired, still dressed in his starched shirt and tie.

"Not when there's work to be done." A typical Carl response. Portraying himself as the servant of the people when in fact he was the master.

"Well, if you do retire, you think you'll come back here?"

"I don't know, Bud. Is that what you're calling about?"

"No." But sometimes I did see the two of us sitting on a porch somewhere, talking about the old days. Despite his faults, and mine, he was my brother. The only family I had. I don't think Carl had many close personal friends either. He knew a lot of people, yes. He couldn't walk a block without half a dozen people stopping him to talk. Still, like me, I think he was lonely. Only the lonely . . .

"Carl?"

"Yes, what is it?"

"Virginia Murphy came by this morning."

"Who's Virginia Murphy?"

"Lila's sister."

I banked on Carl's memory being better than mine. It had been trained for remembering names, faces, the stuff that helped reelect him every term.

"I'm not with you, Bud."

"Lila Murphy. She was killed in 1955. Body found up in Sugarloaf near the bat tower."

Pause.

"Oh, yes. I'd forgotten the name. What's the connection?"

"It was an unsolved murder. Virginia's asked me to look into it."

"After all these years! Why?"

"I don't know. Trying to settle accounts with the past, maybe."

"Is there some new evidence?"

"No."

"What makes her think she's going to learn anything now?"

"Don't know," I said.

"Then why'd you call me?"

"Thought you might remember something, shed some light."

"Sorry to disappoint," Carl replied.

We talked a little more as I stared out the back window at a bunch of kids who had gathered in the weed-covered parking lot. Probably a drug deal going down. Tom came around and rubbed against my ankles, a habit I hated, and I gently shooed him away. After hanging up I went back to the piano. Played around with "Killing Me Softly" once more, then dug the photo of Lila Murphy out of my pocket and laid it on the music rack. Speaking of smiles.

Afterward, I lay down on the bed and read for a while before falling into a dreamless sleep.

At eight-thirty the next morning one of the lawyers from the state attorney's office called with the name of a witness to an accident he needed to talk to. The witness's name was Kenneth Barlow and he lived on Cudjoe Key, twenty-five miles out of Key West. The lawyer had been sending letters and trying to reach Barlow by phone, all without success. Would I go up there and track him down? That's what I was paid for.

I walked around the corner for breakfast in the drugstore on Simonton Street. The drugstore probably offered the last bastion where official Conchdom could gather in one place anymore.

Sweetwater was at the counter when I came in. A black man with a rose tattoo on the huge biceps of one arm, Sweetwater had sparred with Hemingway when the writer was living here in the thirties. He had also worked at City Electric with my father, so Sweetwater had to be at least eighty. Still an imposing figure.

"Bud, how you?" Sweetwater asked as I sat on a stool at the horseshoe counter opposite him.

"Can't complain," I said. "Wouldn't do any good."

"Ain't it the truth."

I spread out my paper and doctored the coffee that one of the waitresses put in front of me before ordering eggs over hard, grits and sausage, and Cuban toast. A gang of City Electric employees filed in and went to the tables in back.

I ate and read and absorbed the familiar smells and sounds of this place where I'd been coming for years. Nodded to Sweetwater when he got up to leave.

Shortly after nine I was on my way up the Keys in the Conchmobile, a 1973 Buick Electra that had taken its share of dings over the years, but still sputtered up and down U.S. 1. The flat seascape with its island hammocks, some old and familiar landmarks mingled with the new, rolled by like a film clip. I kept the windows down, allowing the humid air with its tangy smell to freshen the moldy interior of the car.

Cudjoe Key supposedly got its name from some character known as Cousin Joe, who lived here long ago. Whoever he was. The turnoff at the twenty-six-mile marker was a narrow asphalt road winding back through dense thickets of mangroves to the Atlantic and a scattered residential area of stilt homes built along the water's edge. A numbered mailbox beside the road identified Kenneth Barlow's.

I turned into the dirt lane that led down through a thicket of Australian pines to the house that sat hidden from the road and any distant neighbors.

A car was parked on the open area of concrete beneath the house, which was supported by twelve-foot columns required by the state for homes built this close to the water, for flood protection.

I got out of the Buick and stood in the silence of the place. A hummingbird flitted around the pastel petals of a potted hibiscus plant. I walked up the outside stairway, which led up to a deck and the sliding glass doors that gave entrance to the house. Curtains covered the doors.

I knocked, waited, and knocked again. No answer. I tried the door, which rattled open on its aluminum tracks. Parting the curtains, I stepped inside. "Barlow," I called. Loud enough to be heard throughout the house. Silence.

A long tiled counter divided the kitchen from the dining room in which I was standing. Beyond that was an open living area with more sliding glass doors that looked out over the Atlantic. The far wall to my left had a doorway, which I guessed led to the bedrooms. The place was a dump. Expensive furnishings but magazines and papers were strewn all over, dirty dishes piled everywhere. Ants made continuous tracks along the countertops in the kitchen.

I walked over to the doorway and down a short hall where there were three bedrooms and a bath. The bed in the master bedroom was unmade, with more clothes strewn on the floor than were in the closet. Loose change, cigarettes, bottles of men's cologne turned over on the chest of drawers.

It was hard to tell if the place had been ransacked or its occupants were just poor housekeepers. I walked out on the back deck where there was a charcoal grill filled with gray, cold ash; bits of charred flesh from whatever meat had been cooked there still clung to the rack of the grill. Below me was a narrow cove with a private dock, some lines hanging from it, but no boat.

Along the coast I could see other houses in the distance, but there was a definite feeling of isolation here. I spent another fifteen minutes looking around. Made some notes from the papers I looked through, pocketing several books of matches.

When I left, I pointed the Buick back down the Keys and noticed the trail of blue smoke coming from the exhaust when I tromped the gas. Time for its annual pit stop.

At mile marker seventeen I pulled into the Sugarloaf Lodge for a pit stop of my own. After taking a leak I sat in the bar over a cup of coffee, contemplated the rows of bottles, and decided against a morning drink. Yesterday had been an aberration. I would get myself back on my schedule, one weekend at a time.

Looking out the window, I watched Angel, the pet dolphin, being led through a performance at one of her daily feedings. Shedding water from her sleek skin when she jumped, Angel seemed to stare with one eye directly into the bar at me, the smile etched on her mouth as inscrutable as Mona Lisa's.

I paid for the coffee and left before the show was over. The bat tower was a minute's drive along a dirt road behind the lodge.

The thirty-foot tower built in 1929 looked like a Dutch windmill that was missing its blades. The brainchild of a guy by the name of Clyde Perky, it was designed to combat the mosquito problem by providing a daytime haven for the nocturnal feeders. But nobody bothered to tell the bats, and they never came.

I walked through the stands of sea oats and tall grass wondering exactly where Lila Murphy's body had been found. Apart from the lodge, which was built in 1973, the area wasn't significantly changed from that April night in 1955. I knelt down in the grass and looked up at the sky. One of those long clouds was forming overhead, an early forewarning of the approaching summer.

Alex Farquar, the attorney who had called me that morning, was in court. I walked the short distance from the state attorney's office to the courthouse and took the stairs rather than wait for the elevator, always slow, up to the third floor.

Farquar was a brassy young fellow who looked like he'd just come off an episode of "L.A. Law." He wore wire-rimmed glasses, his dark hair a tangle of curls; his suits always appeared calculatedly rumpled. Of all the attorneys in the office, I disliked working with Farquar the most.

When I came in, he was arguing a point before Judge Watson. Watson, even as a younger man, had always reminded me of Gregory Peck in the movie *To Kill a Mockingbird.* Tall, benevolent, with dark eyes and rather long, tangled hair that was now turning white. He'd been on the bench forever, a family relation by marriage, and a friend.

After Farquar's grandiloquence, the judge, contemplating him with some amusement it seemed to me, ruled in his quiet style, then called for a brief recess. He left the courtroom, nodding in my direction.

Several defendants in their orange prison jumpsuits sat in the jury box awaiting their fates. The bailiff, Earl Summers—we had always called him Early Summers—stood nearby.

"Alex."

Farquar turned. His tie was pulled loose from the blue button-down shirt, the collar button undone. "Gideon. Bearing good news I hope?"

"Afraid not. My opinion Barlow's dusted."

"No, that's not what I want to hear. Tell me."

I described the scene at the house on Cudjoe.

"But the door was open. Wouldn't he have locked it?"

"Maybe, maybe not. Around there you can probably still get by without locking doors." There was a time in Key West when no one locked a door.

"Shit," Farquar said. "Well, stay with it, Gideon. See if you can find out where he's gone at least. We've got a couple weeks on this one."

I said I would and walked toward the jury box, motioning to Early, who smiled and ambled over in the gray and green uniform of the Monroe County sheriff's office, loaded up with black leather around his waist.

"Howdy, Bud."

We shook hands. "Early, I'm looking for Webb. He on today?"

Early stretched a forefinger along the side of his nose. "He might be downstairs. I think he's handin' out subpoenas today."

"Thanks. The clerk's office, right?"

"I'd check there first, then try the dispatcher, case he's on the road."

"Will do."

"Good to see you, Bud."

"Sure thing." I went out and took the stairs down to the second floor to the small office of the clerk of the court.

Wilma Patterson looked up from her computer terminal when I walked in. "Look who the cat drug in," she said.

Wilma and I had been classmates at Key West High. Had even fumbled around in the backseat of a car or two. It wasn't easy to watch what time and trouble could do to us. "Didn't know you missed me."

Wilma scoffed and creased her makeup.

"Looking for Webb Conners," I said.

Wilma looked at the wall clock. "Getting on to lunchtime," she said. "Best look in Yesterday's. You know Webb's not going to be late for a meal."

I grinned and eased out the door.

Yesterday's was a café a block away on Fleming that captured the courthouse crowd. It was new but trying hard to appear like it had been here forever. Webb was tucked into a booth, all 225 pounds of him, also wearing gray and green.

"Mind if I join you?"

"Oh, Bud. Take a load off."

I sat on the hard plastic seat opposite Webb. He was a couple years older than me, had worked for the sheriff's department as a deputy until four or five years ago when his weight and age combined to slow him down. Not ready to quit, he managed to get himself transferred to the less taxing bailiff's position.

"Wha's happ'nin', Bud?" Webb took a bite of his BLT on white bread.

"I'm walking back through the past."

Webb grinned, wiping mayo from his lower lip. "The good old days."

"Were they?"

"Good? I don't know. I guess ever'thing looks good from somebody else's seat."

"I've been trying to figure it." I ordered a chicken salad sandwich from the waitress. "You worked for Frank Paine, didn't you?" I asked Webb when she'd gone.

"Sure. My first administration."

"You remember the Lila Murphy murder?"

"Good God! You diggin' that up?"

"I don't know. Something came up about it. I've been asking questions. I was in Korea when it happened."

"Oh, yeah? I didn't remember that."

I nodded.

"When was it your daddy died?"

"In '58. Two or three years after I got out."

"God, it don't seem possible. The way time flies."

"Webb, were you involved with the Murphy investigation?"

"Not much. Frank handled it, I think. But things were different then, the force was much smaller and I know we all took an interest in it."

The waitress brought my sandwich and potato chips. "You remember anything special about it?"

Webb shrugged. "The way it ended."

"What do you mean?"

"Well, it was on the front burner for a couple of weeks, then it just fizzled out. Nobody even talked about it much."

"The investigation."

"Right."

"Lack of evidence?"

"Yeah, but it was funny. It was almost like they'd decided not to keep it going."

"Any directives? Frank tell people not to pursue it?"

"Not me, but I was a rookie then."

"What'd you think happened?"

"Hell," Webb said. "She was runnin' with the society crowd. I figured somebody pulled rank."

"Deliberate?"

Webb shrugged. "Your guess is as good as mine. You know this town as good as anybody, Bud."

"Yeah," I said. "I guess I do."

10

I can hear my father's voice: "They're your people." It was a favorite expression of his. Meant to insure that I understood, my brother and I both understood, that we Conchs stuck together. Even my mother, I believe, despite her freshwater status, was viewed in subtle ways in the community as an outsider. I'm sure she felt that. Just like I'm sure Captain Billy loved her even while building resentment over her lack of a Conch birthright. To be a Conch was to be favored and in some small way protected, perhaps even forgiven. Almost as if my forefathers had recognized that living on an island we were always subject to invasion.

"You again," Mary Russell said when I walked into the library. "What are you digging into now?"

"Our past."

"Pshaa," Mary rasped. "Trouble more likely."

"The truth will set us free."

"Nothing's going to free the likes of you and me except maybe death. Now what do you want? I'm busy."

"A Conch who's who for the fifties."

"Still pursuing that Murphy girl, eh?"

Mary labored up from her desk, walked to a file cabinet, and took out a folder, which she handed to me. "You should remember these people, Bud. You getting old-timer's disease?"

I whacked her gently on the back with the folder and went to sit down at a table. There was a list of city fathers going back more than a hundred years. I recognized the names, of course, handed down over the years, and some dim recollection of stories told about certain characters.

And, yes, I began to form pictures of the people whose names I read from the decade of Korea and Eisenhower. I jotted the names down on the back of a used library index card. Commissioners were elected every four years to their seat on the city council; mayors every two years. The names of the governing board of the county for those years were less familiar, but I wrote them down, too. Many of these people were dead, some I'd lost track of, but a few, I knew, were still around.

These were the politicians, and politics had always been big on the island. We took who governed us seriously, and until the last couple of decades it had almost always been Conchs. Today of course that had changed; the carpetbaggers had changed it.

There were others—the doctors, lawyers, judges, and bankers—who figured in the upper-scale social fabric of Key West, but by and large Key West society revolved around politics.

They're your people, Captain Billy said.

I took my list to Mary. "How many of us are still alive?" I asked.

"Can't speak for you, but me and a half dozen of these folks still put our feet on the floor in the morning."

"Any one of them that might have been more tuned into the social whirl back then?"

"Oh, they all were. You know how we loved to party."

"I know. I was thinking about the Garden of Palms just the other day."

"Nothing like that around anymore," Mary said. "Bud, you should talk to Doc Westerby. He was part of that high-society crowd. He loves to talk about it, and his memory's still good."

"Thanks, I'll call him."

"You really think you're going solve that murder, Bud?"

"Don't know," I said. "It can't hurt to ask a few questions."

"Yeah, until you start digging up old skeletons."

"You think I might do that?"

"There's plenty of them around."

We were like one large family here, truly an extension of our immediate families, and I suppose we wanted, like any other family, to keep our skeletons in the closet.

I walked the few blocks back to the courthouse where the Buick was parked. I was about to get in it when I thought of something and went back to the courthouse, to the county public-records department. A host of young women worked there; by their accents I judged most of them were Conchs, but I didn't know them. I asked one dark-haired beauty if she could show me the property descriptions for Cudjoe Key. She disappeared and came back moments later with a large ledger, which she put on the counter, then helped me locate the property I wanted. It was listed in the name of Kenneth Barlow, who had purchased it in 1992. Taxes were paid up and no liens were recorded.

A lot of those houses up the Keys had been built by

carpetbaggers with drug money. After legitimate avenues of getting rich failed, many saw in the Keys easy pickings for less traditional methods of work. That's not to say "my people" avoided those routes, but in the late sixties and early seventies the Johnny-come-latelies brought an ingenuity to the smuggling profession that had been unnecessary for the Conchs. Until the feds got actively into the action the locals could usually depend upon the "bubba system" to protect them; they would bring their hauls via shrimp boats straight to the dock. Outsiders depended on the narrow, shallow channels up the Keys, and speedboats, to maneuver the cargo from the larger ships anchored out. Later, planes were used, landing on small, desolate runways around here and south Florida until finally, ten years or so ago, the smuggling adventure pretty much ground to a halt in the Keys with Reagan's drug wars and the advances in surveillance technology.

But not before a lot of people were living legitimate lives on illegitimate gain. I wondered if Kenneth Barlow was one of them.

I drove the Buick home and called Doc Westerby who seemed pleased to hear from me. He invited me over at the cocktail hour, six o'clock, for a drink.

11

Hal Westerby lived in new town, a ranch-style home off Flagler Avenue on Riviera Drive. A front lawn with grass, a two-car garage, one car in the driveway. It was a picture of suburban America in the fifties before town houses and condos. It was what my generation of people aspired to, to get out of those old, drafty wooden houses and move up to air-conditioning—which as much as television, I believe, spoiled successive generations.

Doc Westerby wasn't a Conch. He came here as a navy doctor during the war and soon after retired from the military to start a private practice in Key West. He told me all that while escorting me through the house to the screened-in Florida room overlooking a fenced-in yard —more grass—and a canal.

Tall, slightly slope-shouldered now, Westerby had iron gray hair, a large, red nose, and the air of a medical man. He wore a beige lounge suit.

The Florida room was clearly where most of the living went on at the Westerbys. A worn rattan sofa, a couple of La-Z-Boy rocking chairs, stacks of magazines in baskets on the floor, pictures of the grandkids on the walls and end tables, and some hanging plants.

The bar was a portable double-deck tray on rollers, the bottles stacked on the lower tray, the ice bucket, glasses, and mixers on the top. There was nothing a drinking man wouldn't find here.

"Name your poison," Westerby said jovially.

Poison indeed. I eyed the rum bottle. "Club soda," I replied.

"Ah, a nondrinker. That seems to be the fashion these days." Westerby fixed my soda in an old-fashioned glass, with a deft squeeze of lemon, then filled the same kind of glass with ice, pouring it full with Johnnie Walker Red. "Different generation," he added, raising his glass.

We toasted; I felt chided. Westerby was seventy-five but looked ten years younger. He offered a seat and I chose the couch over one of the La-Z-Boys.

"When you mentioned Lila Murphy, I took the liberty of inviting my old friend Paul Murchison over. You know him?"

The name was familiar but I couldn't place it.

"He was the medical examiner back then," Westerby said.

Oh, yes. "That's fine," I said. "You remember Lila?"

Westerby rolled his eyes. "Oh, boy, do I. She was a knockout."

"She was just out of high school though, wasn't she?"

It was Westerby's turn to look rebuked since he would have been close to forty at the time Lila was killed.

"Well, she was a classy kid. She ran with a somewhat older crowd, but I remember her from some of the dances back then."

"Were you at that last dance? At the Elks club."

Westerby sipped his Scotch. "Of course. It was just another dance and I wouldn't have remembered it except we were all questioned by the police."

"Anything stand out in your memory about Lila that night?"

"No, they asked all of us who were there that question, and nothing came to mind. There was talk that she was drinking at the bar with a stranger, but I didn't see him."

"You dance with her?"

Westerby laughed. "I don't think I did that night. Maybe at other dances I did once or twice, but as you pointed out, I was quite a bit older. She was mostly with the young professionals coming up. And I was married."

"And still are," a woman said.

I turned and got to my feet. Mrs. Westerby came over and introduced herself. She had on a print dress belted around the waist, nylons, which one seldom saw in this town anymore, and looked as if she'd just come from the hairdresser's.

Westerby offered to fix her a drink when the doorbell rang.

"I'll get it," Ann Westerby said. "Fix me the usual."

"It's Paul," Hal replied. He went to the bar and mixed a gin and tonic while Ann answered the door.

When she came back she was with a tall, exceedingly thin man with a hawk nose and thick glasses, nearly bald. Westerby introduced Paul Murchison. We shook hands and I could feel the bones barely covered by flesh.

Ann took her drink and sat on the couch. There was an easy familiarity among the three of them. Westerby fixed another Scotch for Paul and the two men sat in the La-Z-Boys. These were not my people.

"Gideon's been asking about the Lila Murphy murder." Westerby spoke more loudly as though his friend might be hard of hearing.

Murchison nodded in my direction. "Oh, yes. Interesting case."

"You were the medical examiner then?" I followed Westerby's lead and raised my voice.

"Until 1970." Murchison took a long pull of Scotch.

"You remember what the cause of death was?"

"Apparently from a blow to the head."

"I wonder if they keep autopsy reports back that far?" I asked.

"It wouldn't make any difference," Murchison said, "because there wasn't an autopsy."

"I didn't know that," Westerby responded with some surprise.

"The family didn't want it," Murchison said.

"I can understand that," Ann said. "Such a gruesome thing to go through."

"But you didn't establish an exact cause of death," I said.

Murchison shifted slightly in the La-Z-Boy. "Well, it

was apparent that the blow to the back of her head was sufficient to cause death."

"Is that normal?"

Murchison shrugged. "It was the way things were done back then. We tried to follow the wishes of the family."

"Who in the family did you talk to?"

Murchison finished his Scotch. "Actually I didn't talk to them directly. It came from the authorities."

"Which ones?"

"The sheriff, I guess."

"Frank Paine?"

"I suppose so," Murchison said.

Westerby got up to refresh their drinks. I hung around for another half hour and watched them all get slightly addled talking about the good times of the past.

▼▼▼▼

12

▼▼▼▼

The rest of the week I spent running into dead ends. Everyone I wanted to talk to was either in the hospital, not answering their phone, or out of town. Anyone else might have gotten paranoid and decided there was a conspiracy to avoid me. I tried to take it in stride. I knew I was dealing with age, and in some cases the infirm, and patience was required. Even Virginia Murphy seemed to have disappeared.

Until Thursday. Around noon that day I was at my desk looking over some of the documents I'd copied from the library, going over more names from the past, when the phone rang. It was Virginia.

"I came by Big Betty's a couple times looking for you," I said.

"I'm sorry. I had to go away for a while."

"I wanted to talk to you about Lila."

"I don't know. Maybe it was wrong of me to come here digging this up again. What good will it do?"

I thought of what I'd said to Mary Russell in jest the other day. The truth will set us free. But I wasn't sure I believed that. Not in Virginia's case. She was too haunted.

"We should talk," I said. "Shall I come there?"

Virginia hesitated.

I pressed her: "It's important."

"I'll come to you then."

"You remember where I am?"

"I'll get a taxi. I can be there in ten minutes."

She came in the front door in less than ten minutes. She seemed a little calmer than the last time we'd met, her face looked better although she was still wearing the nun's habit that revealed so little of her physical features. Her hands, however, seemed steadier as she sat down in the wicker chair in front of the desk. I did not make the mistake of offering her a drink.

"You're looking well," I said.

A hint of a smile crossed her thin lips, then disappeared. "I went up to Miami and checked myself in the hospital for three days after I saw you. I have to do that once in a while."

A drying-out clinic. I felt sympathy for this woman. We both had our ways of trying to keep control over a disease that sooner or later would probably prove stronger than either of us. She knew it; I knew it.

"How long does it last? The cure."

She turned her hands up. "One just never knows. I live in hope."

I nodded. "But sober you're ready to stop looking into the past."

"Do you have reason to believe it's worth continuing?"

"I think there's plenty of reason. I think Lila's death was hushed up and there's a good possibility there are people in this town still alive who know why."

Virginia studied me silently, her face betraying no emotion, and it was impossible to know what she might be thinking. Finally, she said, "You wanted to ask me about Lila."

"I was hoping you could tell me something about your life here."

Virginia sighed. "It was difficult. Apart from what happened to Lila."

"In what way difficult?"

"Well, we were new here. We had been uprooted from our home in Savannah. It was hard making new friends."

Yes, we do not open our arms to strangers easily. "It's true we tend to be close-knit," I said.

"Oh, it's not just you. Key West. It's the South. We are so protective. We knew that and I suppose we knew we would have to try extra hard to be accepted."

"And did you?"

"It was easier for Lila. She was more attractive, more outgoing than I am."

"Especially with boys?" I asked gently.

Virginia nodded.

"Any particular boys that you remember?"

Virginia looked away, glancing at the bare walls, reaching down to stroke Tom, who had come in from the kitchen.

"I know this is difficult for you," I said. "But it's important."

"Lila could have had any boy she wanted. They were all after her."

"But she didn't want them, did she?"

Virginia shook her head. "No, she liked older men."

"Did you and Lila ever go out together?"

"Not very often. Sometimes we would find ourselves in the same place, but usually not together."

"Did Lila not want you around?"

"I was the younger sister."

I felt like a shrink with these questions and I could see Virginia drawing away. I sensed that I wouldn't be able to press her further without losing her all together.

"Will you do something for me?" I asked.

Virginia just looked at me without answering.

"Will you think about the people Lila hung out with, see if you can remember any names, or anything about them that would help me identify her boyfriends?"

Virginia pressed her hands together. "I'll try."

"If you want me to go on with this, I need you to do that."

She said she would think about it and stood up, seeming to be relieved that this was over. When she left, I watched her walk up the street, like a vapor, disappearing in the heat. I wasn't sure I would ever see her again, she had so reduced herself, hidden behind the shadow of her dead sister.

13

I was wrong. On Friday I was back playing at the Club, and drinking. It was the weekend. She came in as before, toward the end of the first set. I finished up with "As Time Goes By," then joined Virginia at the bar. Ronnie handed me a fresh Barbancourt.

Virginia seemed tired, distant. I would have bet that she'd spent a sleepless night after our talk yesterday. It was clear that she had been devastated by her sister's death. Why she had never recovered after all this time was a question perhaps only a shrink could answer. I waited while she stared out the darkened windows behind the bar before turning to me.

"You said yesterday you thought there was reason to believe Lila's death had been hushed up. What makes you think that?"

"Because there was no autopsy." I tasted my drink. "Did your family not want one performed?"

"I don't really remember."

"The medical examiner at the time said it was at the family's request."

Virginia seemed to stare into that middle distance where the past resided. After a moment, she said, "We were all in deep shock. I do remember the sheriff coming to talk to my parents several times."

"That was Frank Paine."

Virginia shrugged. "Is he still alive?"

"No."

"Lila had been struck on the head, that was the cause of death, wasn't it?"

"Maybe it was. But it's odd there was no autopsy."

"And you believe it was deliberate?"

I nodded.

We lapsed into silence again until I asked if she'd thought any more about what we'd talked about yesterday.

"About Lila's boyfriends?"

"Or the men she seemed drawn to."

"There were just so many, and you forget names after all these years."

I felt discouraged. I'd been hoping for a breakthrough, some small lead that would have provided a clue to Lila's social life. "What about you?" I asked. "Were there boys in your life then?"

Virginia raised a hand to her face. "Me?" she asked with an expression of incredulity. "Oh, no. They were all interested in Lila."

And there it was. The unattractive girl who felt insignificant beside her beautiful sister, a shadowy figure who remained shrouded and ghostlike, doomed to a life of inaction. Something in me hoped that Virginia would not want to go on with this, since I suspected that nothing that could possibly be revealed after all this time, even Lila's killer, would release Virginia from her torment.

As if reading my mind, Virginia said, "I've decided I want you to continue with your investigation."

"Even though it may raise more difficult questions for you, and in the end answer nothing."

Virginia studied me. "I have accepted that. And I trust you."

I nodded. "I get a hundred dollars a day, plus expenses. We'll call it three days for this week. No expenses."

"I recall a bottle of rum."

"You go to a clinic. I buy my own booze."

Virginia reached into a slender white bag on the bar and withdrew a checkbook. I watched her write out a check for two thousand dollars in a not-quite-steady hand. "Will this keep you going for a while?" she asked, handing it to me.

"You planning on being gone again?"

"You never know in this life, do you?"

"No, you never do."

Harry was returning to the stage, back from his break. He sat down and began tuning up. I stood up. Virginia put her hand in mine as though we'd just met or were saying good-bye. "Thank you, Gideon."

"I haven't done anything."

"No, but you will. I can see it in your eyes. I trust you."

I felt embarrassed, withdrew, and went to the piano. My refuge. Where I tried to do some Gershwin, making a hash of "They Can't Take That Away From Me." My phrasing was off. I got away from Gershwin, following it with something easier. "Old Devil Moon."

I didn't see Virginia leave. Ronnie kept sending drinks over, and I was aware I wasn't pacing myself. I felt lousy, a failure, but masked it with bonhomie between sets, razzing Harry and the others while continuing to throw down the rum.

I got home after three with Virginia's check in my pocket and a buzz in my head. When I opened the door, Tom must have been waiting there. I stepped on his paw. He yelped and scrambled for the desk drawer. I turned on lights and thought about a nightcap before trying to sleep, thinking it would help, and of course it would only do the opposite unless I drank enough to pass out.

Which I suppose I did. I woke at eleven the next morning, hung over, my mouth dry as a canyon bed, and stumbled up to feed the cat. Then I went back to bed and tried to get up at noon. I made coffee, turning on the radio for distraction.

The news was of a woman who'd taken a tumble down the stairs at Big Betty's guesthouse. Somehow I knew even though no name was given. You never know in this life, do you? Virginia Murphy said. My hand trembled as I reached for the bottle of Barbancourt to pour a splash in my coffee.

I didn't know the two cops who came to the door at one-thirty. I had lost contact with the department years ago. I suppose it's a byproduct of age, but the cops today all looked so young and fresh-faced it was hard to imagine them in any way threatening. You just wanted to chuck them under the chin.

I was still in recovery. My hands trembled and nervous tics pinched the corners of my eyes. I picked up a pair of dusty sunglasses from the top of one of the filing cabinets and put them on before opening the door.

"Mr. Lowry?" one of the plainclothes officers asked. His voice tentative; even, I thought, respectful.

I didn't trust my own voice and merely nodded; the midday sun bouncing off Duval Street hurt my eyes even behind the shades.

"Mind if we come in?"

I did mind, but I was unable to protest. I opened the door a little wider and let the two kids in. Really neither one of them could have been more than twenty-five. They wore jeans, black sneakers, and tropical shirts. One was blond; the other had long brown hair. In the old days he would have been required to get a haircut.

I motioned toward the chairs in front of my desk and then walked back to my apartment. The rum was on the kitchen counter. I hated myself for it but I took two long pulls straight from the bottle. Of course it was a losing battle, but I still had good intentions of winning the war. I steadied myself, breathing deeply, before walking back into the office. I sat down behind the desk and kept my hands wrapped around the chair arms while the boy cops stared at me like I was some kind of freak.

"Talk to me," I grunted.

The blond coughed. "A woman died over at Big Betty's last night. Did you hear about it?"

"Yeah. 'S on the radio."

"Virginia Murphy."

I nodded.

Blondie was rubbing his hands together. "Well, we've been asking questions—"

"This a murder investigation?" I had to work to frame the question.

"Just a preliminary inquiry into what appears to be an accidental death," Longhair said.

Shit.

"We heard Ms. Murphy hung out at the Club," Blondie interjected.

"Twice that I know about. Wouldn't call it hanging out."

"She was there last night?"

I nodded.

Blondie was having a hard time in this role, but I liked him better than I did his partner, who I tried to ignore. Of course the only person I really didn't like was myself.

"You talk to her?"

I nodded again. Not making it easy for him, but I was fighting off nausea. I could feel my face break into a sweat. I wanted another drink. I wanted to curl up in the dark of my cave and never come out. I wanted the world to stop spinning and let me off. I was found wanting. That was the truth.

"You okay, Mr. Lowry?"

I tried to grin through clenched teeth.

"We heard she was a boozer," Longhair said.

I felt the blood begin to surge up to my face. "No!" I said loudly. "She hadn't had a drink in four days." With a growl that was almost human, Tom scrambled from the desk drawer and shot out of the kitchen through the hole I'd cut in the back door for him.

Blondie was clearly ill at ease now. "It's okay, Mr. Lowry."

Mr. Lowry. These jackasses must see me with one foot in the grave, I thought.

"Were you working for her? Someone saw her write you a check."

I took a deep breath. "Still working for her."

"Do you want to tell us about that?"

"I don't." Not that I wouldn't, but right now I couldn't get the words out.

Blondie stood up and Longhair followed. I remained in my seat, clenching the armrests. The two of them backed toward the front door. "See yourselves out," I mumbled. The glass in the door rattled when they closed it, a sound that shattered my nerves. I just made it to the bathroom before I blew.

When it was over, I came out and sat down at the kitchen table with the bottle and a glass. The glass was a step in the right direction. With the back of my hand I wiped at the tears that dripped from behind the dark glasses. I had drunk myself from self-loathing into self-pity. Somehow I had to find my way back.

The phone rang a few times during the afternoon, but I didn't answer it. I didn't bother to pick up the mail when the mailman stuffed it through the slot in the front door. I just sat in the darkness of the back room and mulled over the past. The future seemed hardly worth considering. In my beginning is my end. I loved my mother because she had the good sense to give me poetry and music. Which is how I dealt with Captain Billy's death, I suppose. And would be how I dealt with everyone else's dying, including Virginia Murphy.

The sun was waning when I came out of it. Tom returned home and lingered around the kitchen until I fed him. I took a shower and put on a fresh pair of khaki pants and a clean white shirt. Held my hands out in front of me for a seismic reading. If I could get a meal in me and hold it down, I thought I would be able to play tonight. I might have to have a drink to get through the night, but I vowed to make it only one.

And to go by Big Betty's before going to the Club.

15

We have the reputation of being a live-and-let-live kind of town. I'm not sure it's a reputation totally deserved. Some of my people have had a hard time adjusting to the notion that Key West attracts a lot of society's fringe. Sadly, the gay community has come in for its share of prejudice over the years. Plenty of jokes went around about Big Betty's.

I don't know what I expected when I went in, but no one came over and spat on me. The woman at the reception desk actually smiled. Given my appearance, I thought that must have taken courage.

"A friend of mine was staying here," I said.

"Recently?"

"Until last night."

The smile disappeared, replaced by a look of sadness. "Virginia?"

I nodded.

"I'm sorry," she said. I was sure that she meant it.

"So am I." I introduced myself and explained that I'd also been working for Virginia, asking if I could see the room where she'd stayed.

"My name's Jane." She offered her pudgy hand. Jane was probably in her forties and overweight. "There's nothing in the room. The police took everything."

"Why did they do that? Wasn't her death an accident?"

"I guess they're investigating, and looking for any relatives."

"I don't think she had any. At least not close ones."

"I'm happy to show you the room." Jane took some keys from the rack behind the desk and called for someone to watch the front.

The stairway led up from the front door to a second-floor landing. The banister was heavy polished wood with a sculpted mermaid on top of the newel post, her posterior rubbed smooth where she'd been grabbed over the years by people starting up the stairs. On the way up I counted nineteen steps. There was no elevator.

"Were you working last night?" I asked Jane.

"After eleven o'clock there's no one on the front desk. The door is locked and guests have their own keys."

"Do staff stay in the building?"

"I'm the owner. I have an apartment in the back with my lover and partner, but we live separately from the main part of the guesthouse. The rest of the staff live out."

"Who found Virginia?" We were standing now on the landing, looking down at the bottom of the steps.

"Two guests coming in after her."

"What time was that?"

"About two-thirty this morning. Everyone staying here has my home phone number. The two women who found Virginia called me. I got up, came out, and called an ambulance and the police."

"Did you have any reason to believe it was anything more than an accident?"

"I didn't know what happened. I have to take every precaution in this business."

"Was Virginia already dead?"

"I think so."

"Did she have any friends here, hang out with anyone?"

"No, she was very much a loner. The common misconception is that everybody here is having an orgy every night. That isn't true. I liked Virginia, we talked a few times, but only in passing. She wasn't with anyone."

"How many rooms?"

"Ten."

"All occupied?"

"Yes."

"And no one saw anything or heard a commotion?"

"No. Most of the guests were in bed and slept through the whole thing. A few were still out on the town." Jane turned away from the stairway. "Virginia had this corner room."

Number two. The door was five steps back from the landing at the entrance to a narrow, carpeted hallway. The door opened into the room. I went in behind Jane.

It was a large room with a brass bed, an antique marble-topped dresser and tables. Old-fashioned. There was a small private bathroom adjoining the room with small framed prints of women on the walls.

"Did the cops talk to your other guests?"

"Yes. They were here a couple hours this morning."

I stepped back into the hallway. It would have been easy the way the door opened for someone to approach silently along the carpeted hall while Virginia was unlocking her door and shove her hard enough to push her down the stairs only a few steps from the door. Virginia couldn't have weighed much more than ninety pounds.

I knew of course it was also possible Virginia had brought someone back here with her. And equally possible that she'd resumed drinking and taken a fall without any outside assistance.

"She went away for a few days," I said to Jane. "Did you notice any difference when she came back?"

"You mean the drinking?"

I nodded. "She went to a clinic in Miami she told me. She wasn't drinking the last time I was with her."

Jane shook her head. "I think she was drinking again. There was an odor of alcohol when I got to her."

So the cure was short-lived. Virginia had lost her battle, and it had cost her her life. As we walked back down the stairs, I wondered if my questioning her and the discussion of the autopsy might have been too much, more than that tormented soul could withstand.

I stood with my hand resting on the mermaid. "If you think of anything at all, I'd appreciate a call," I said. "I'm sorry, I don't use business cards."

"Gideon Lowry. I'll remember."

I went out and walked down Smith Lane and around the corner to the Club. Thankfully, it was nearly empty. I asked Ronnie if she remembered serving drinks to the woman in white I had been talking to last night. Ronnie said, yes, Virginia had been drinking. I went to the piano and led off the first set with "Sentimental Journey." And I didn't keep my other vow.

16

There was a familiar knock at the back door. *Bah baba bah ba. Bah bah.* Casey. Shirtless, I came out of the bathroom, where I'd been trying to get the bottom of the birdcage out of my mouth, and saw her through the glass. She gave a wave, holding her hand up and opening and closing her fingers against her palm the way she did. I opened the door and let her in, stepping away so that she wouldn't try to kiss me and be repelled by whatever lingered on my breath. I should have known that she already knew, which was why she was here.

"I hear you've been hitting the bottle again pretty hard," Casey said, sitting down at the kitchen table. She was in her midforties, a tall, silvery blonde with a wonderful disposition and an infectious laugh. A small cluster of crow's-feet edged her light blue eyes, and two half-moon-like wrinkles creased her face at the corners of her mouth. She bore a certain resemblance to Jane Fonda, I thought.

I'd known Casey Syms for twenty years. We'd had an on-again, off-again relationship for the past ten, recently mostly off. Casey was an alcoholic who hadn't had a drink in twelve years. She went to AA meetings regularly and without badgering encouraged me to come if I ever decided I needed help. If I had, we might have solidified something over the years, but each of us seemed to hold back; Casey, I think, because she wasn't sure she wanted to get so involved with a drinker, and a man nearly fifteen years older than she.

"The word's out, is it?" I went to the stove, struck a match, and held it to the front burner. My hand trembled, but I didn't feel that bad. I seemed to have leveled off.

"The coconut telegraph," Casey said, referring to Key West's rumor mill.

"Coffee?"

"Please."

I welcomed the distraction. Nondrinkers could be insufferable in the morning.

"Good to see you," I said. "Been a while."

"Three weeks, a month?" Casey said. Tom came in and jumped up in her lap, the flirt.

"What have you been up to?"

"Working."

Casey was an illustrator and a graphic artist. A good one. She always seemed to have plenty of work from the ad trade here.

"You seeing anyone?" Casey dated, and she discussed it with me, told me about the difficulties in this town of hanging on to relationships. I sometimes wondered if I'd become a father figure for her. But right now it was all distraction; by talking about her we avoided talking about me.

"No one in particular." Which meant she wasn't sleeping with anyone because she had always said she could only be involved with one man at a time. In between, we would sometimes start up again.

I took Casey her coffee. "Can we talk about you now, Bud?" she said. Could it be that for me Casey was a mother figure? Like Phyllis, Casey had come to Key West from the outside; she'd come with an education and a strong sense of purpose. She just hadn't met her Captain Billy yet. Or had she? In many ways I was of course my father. A night of drinking could produce such thoughts.

"What's there to talk about?"

"Your drinking."

Why do I drink? God, let me count the reasons. But of course there was no place to begin. I told Casey about Virginia Murphy.

When I finished, we sat in silence for a while. Then Casey asked, "What are you going to do?"

"About Virginia? I don't know."

"I was thinking about her sister, Lila."

I didn't know about that either. A forty-year-old crime and no client. There was a two-thousand-dollar check still sitting in my desk drawer. I could tear it up and forget about it. Virginia wouldn't have wanted that, but I had no obligations to the dead. On the other hand, maybe I did. I thought of Phyllis and Captain Billy and all those Lowrys lying in the cemetery.

"I'll pursue it," I said.

Casey nodded and dumped Tom from her lap. Then came over and knelt beside my chair, resting her head against my bare chest. "If I can help," she murmured.

I put my arm around her shoulders and caressed her. Casey turned her head into me and found one of my nipples with her mouth. Ah. I reached down and stroked the bare flesh of her thighs. Five minutes of that and we got up and went to the other room and spent Sunday in bed. I didn't take a drink, so Casey, knowingly I'm sure, had already started to be of help.

17

It has been said that politics is the lifeblood of Monroe County. At least it was once. Today, most of the old faces are gone; few Conchs get elected to office anymore as the single-issue candidates get voted in for a term, only to be replaced four years later by the next Johnny-come-lately. The political dynasties of the past are dead. I think of the Villani family and the Bayards, who dominated Key West politics for almost half a century.

The Villanis worked mostly behind the scenes, promoting candidates outside their family, ones who would be loyal to the Villani agenda. The Villanis were Old World patrician. Originally from Spain, they had come to Key West in the thirties, bought a lot of downtown commercial property, which they got for a song, probably paying no more than what each property's monthly lease payment would be today. The Villani family was shrewd but noble. They gave back in charity; they contributed to public parks; they helped, without publicity, the poor and disadvantaged. In short, they were what all communities needed and few got. Not surprisingly, I suppose, their political candidates invariably were Democrats—who usually challenged the Republican Bayards.

The Bayards were old Conchs, but relatively new money. They had been wreckers in the days when salvaging cargo from shipwrecks off the reefs could make a man instantly rich. But most of the Bayard wealth came in later years from the concrete business. They owned a quarry up the Keys that supplied Monroe County developers with the only cement-mixing business south of Miami. The Bayards entered the political fray like sharks to blood.

Unlike the Villanis, the Bayards were many and noisy. Whatever they did they made sure they received the maximum publicity. A social gathering wasn't complete unless the Bayards' picture appeared in the newspaper the following day. They didn't just stay in city politics either. For a few years they had family on every county board there was. And old John T. Bayard, now dead, was a state senator for many years.

The man my brother, Carl, had once worked for as a Senate aide.

Carl and I both went to school with Bayards. Carl's closest friends in fact were two of the three Bayard sons. Peter, the eldest, was Carl's age, and they had been close when they were in school together. Peter Bayard broke with family tradition by becoming an architect. Not a particularly good one, I've heard, but any public buildings that were being renovated, Peter was generally awarded the contract. And of course the buildings all got the maximum in concrete.

I didn't know the Villanis, who lived quietly at one end of town, on the Atlantic side in a stately mansion; the Bayards lived lavishly on the Gulf side, and I knew them because, as Captain Billy said, they were our people. I didn't trust them.

Peter still practiced architecture from his office just off Duval on Southard Street. He only worked half days, ten to two, and I managed to get a ten-o'clock appointment when I called his secretary at nine.

I walked in at ten; Peter was late. His secretary smiled sweetly and offered me a seat next to a rock pond complete with gushing water. I suppose it was better than canned music. I picked up a copy of *Architectural Digest* and sat down.

There were no windows in the large, open reception area, and I could as easily have been in the desert Southwest as the Florida Keys, I thought. Little outcroppings of brick on the textured concrete walls reminded me of footholds for rock climbers. As I looked through the *Digest,* they also reminded me of Frank Lloyd Wright, whose design for Florida Southern College in Lakeland was featured in a photo layout. I wondered if Peter Bayard, lacking talents of his own, had perhaps borrowed from the master.

At ten-twenty the secretary told me Peter had arrived and I could go in. The front door hadn't opened since I'd come in, the phone didn't ring, and I hadn't heard an intercom. Perhaps they had some extrasensory communication at work here. Or maybe he'd been in there all the time.

I stepped into Peter's office. Standing beside a large desk, Peter Bayard looked much older than in the many photos I'd seen of him in the *Key West Citizen.* The skin across his face was tight, like it might have been stretched. Surgery, I suspected. Absent any photos, he was probably thinking I didn't look so good either. But it wasn't due to cosmetic surgery. I couldn't remember when we'd last met, but it had been a long while.

"Bud, you're looking well."

The thing I didn't like about the Bayards was their habit of thinking one thing and saying another. And I knew they did that the way I knew ugly caterpillars turned into butterflies. The Bayards were consumed by social correctness. Appearances. I didn't say anything in return, just shook Peter's hand.

"What do I owe the pleasure?" Peter asked, motioning to a chair in front of his clean, elegant desk. I sat down. Peter walked over to a watercooler and drizzled water into a cone-shaped paper cup. He offered it to me. I shook my head. "You want coffee? I can have my secretary get us a couple of *buches* from the Cuban place down the street."

"I'm fine."

Peter downed his water and came back to the desk. He carefully pinched his gray slacks at the knees as he sat down. His silk tie was knotted at his throat, and I'd seen a blue blazer hanging on a coatrack by the door when I came in. This from a man descended from wreckers.

"So," Peter said, settling in.

"I'm working on an old case."

"Hmmm. Come to think of it, I have heard something recently. A murder?"

"Yes, Lila Murphy."

"That's it."

"You remember her?"

"Oh, not so well. I don't think I knew her. But the murder, yes."

"You might have been at the dance the night she disappeared. You and your brother."

Jack was the next oldest, a year or two younger than I, and the Bayard who in adult years claimed more of my brother's attention within the political arena. Jack ran the cement business. Clint was the youngest Bayard, a wild one who a few years ago was rumored to be heavy into drugs but whom I hadn't heard much about recently. There were also a couple of sisters, but in this male-oriented family we never seemed to hear as much about them.

"Oh, well, probably," Peter said.

"You don't remember the police asking questions?"

"I can't say that I do."

Why? Because the cops wouldn't have questioned a Bayard, dragging them through anything as unpleasant as a murder investigation back then. Not Frank Paine anyway, who would have been indebted to John T. Bayard for his job. That's the way I saw it.

"I was trying to remember the other day," I said, "when it was that Carl went up to Tallahassee to work with your father."

"Sometime around then. We graduated from high

school in '48 and went to college in Tallahassee. Carl wanted to get into politics and never finished college, talking my father into a job. What do you hear from him, Bud?"

"Talked to him the other night. He's hanging in." Although Peter and Carl were close friends while they were growing up, in their adult years it was Jack whom Carl had grown closer to.

"Going to run again?"

"Probably."

Peter smiled. Running for office was just a formality for Carl since he hadn't been opposed in years. "Look at us," Peter exclaimed. "The last of a breed."

I didn't care to be included in that sentiment and said nothing.

"You still playing piano?" Peter's eyes twinkled.

A piano player and a private cop was the Bayard way of putting me in my place. "I'm at the Club on the weekends."

"Oh, yes. We'll have to come up one night."

"Do that. I play the old songs." Peter smiled and I stood up. "Also, anything stirs your memory about the Murphy case, let me know."

"Of course."

I was at the door when I thought of something else. "Clint around? I never hear much about him anymore."

Peter let his eyes shift to the desk. "He's working with Jack at the plant."

I nodded and went out. The secretary smiled sweetly again when I left, stepping into the Key West present.

18

The police station was a short walk from Peter Bayard's office, cutting through Key Lime Square. It was in a cinderblock building on Angela Street that housed one of the fire stations, the police, and some city offices.

As a young cop I'd worked out of the old city hall building, which had recently been renovated, over on Greene Street. It was there that I had learned of Captain Billy's death. This building wasn't constructed until sometime in the sixties. Landmarks. I still often got my bearings in this town by buildings and establishments that no longer exist; except in my mind.

I went up to the second floor and knocked on the door with Capt. George Lewis's name on it. A voice said, "Come in!" and I opened the door.

George was sitting behind his desk in the small office. "Well, well, well," he said, "would you look-it who's here. The bad boy himself."

"Those guys caught me on an off day."

George laughed. He was in his midfifties, the chief of detectives. And one of the last of the Conchs in the KWPD. "They thought you were going to puke on 'em."

"I had the courtesy to wait until they left."

George laughed again. "How you feel today?"

"Better than I did yesterday. Why didn't you come yourself? Why'd you send two green kids over?"

"They need the experience, Bud."

"I'm not a goddamn training field."

"Now, Bud, don't get hot under the collar. No pain, no gain, as we say."

"Shit! What have you got on the Murphy death? What'd you find in her room?"

"Whoa! Hold up there, my friend. This isn't a one-way street. You gave my boys nothing. Now you want us to play by your rules. Shame on you, Bud."

"There was nothing to tell those guys."

"The woman gave you a check. You were working for her. Now she's dead. I think you can tell me something."

"She had a sister who was killed here in the fifties. Unsolved. She asked me to look into it."

George whistled. "I think that's relevant information."

"Maybe, maybe not. Depends on the nature of Virginia's death."

"We don't know that. She definitely died from the fall she took. Why? You think she was pushed?"

"I'm keeping an open mind," I said. "You letting the boys handle the investigation?"

George eyed me across the desk. "They're questioning the women at Big Betty's. Don't worry. I've been over there and walked them through the prelim."

"What about her stuff?"

"There wasn't much. Some clothes, the usual toiletries. A couple of books."

"What did you do with it?"

"We're trying to establish kin. She was from Savannah, and so far that's all we know. We were just hoping, Bud, that you could help us."

"From the way those guys came on the other day, it sounded more like you thought I killed her."

"Don't exaggerate, Bud. You were just hung over. You gonna pursue the old murder?"

"I'm pursuing everything. I can't retire because I'd

just sit around and drink myself to death, so I got to keep working."

"Everybody's got to die of somethin'," George said, grinning.

I stood up and went to the door. "How do you get along with the chief?" A new police chief had taken over the year before, and rumor had it he was cleaning the stables.

"Hey, I do my job and stay out of his way. So far so good. Let's have a drink together sometime."

"I quit this morning."

"Sure, but I was thinking more of an evening."

George Lewis's laughter followed me down the hallway.

According to the clock downstairs in the lobby, it was almost noon when I went outside. I cut through the back streets and lanes, avoiding Duval Street until the last minute. Avoiding the hordes of people, nameless faces that now patrolled my town.

Back at the office there was a message from Alex Farquar. And mail. Bills, circulars, and two letters, one from the city. I opened it. A contractor had applied for a permit to build a motel on the parking lot that I thought of as my backyard. Did I have any objections? Damned right I had objections. But would it make any difference?

The other letter was an invitation to play at a dance being held in a couple of weeks. A charity ball being sponsored by the Villani family to raise money for the protection of the reef. Another fading landmark.

I sat down at the desk and reached for the phone book. I looked up the Villanis' number, called, and spoke to Portia Villani, the matriarch. I told her that I would be happy to play at the dance. Then I asked if I could pay a visit. I had some questions about an incident from the past she might be able to help me with. Portia invited me over at one o'clock.

When I hung up, I walked to the drugstore for a sandwich, avoiding Alex Farquar, who I knew was going to press me about Kenneth Barlow. Barlow wasn't on my A list right now.

19

The Villani mansion occupied the corner of Whitehead and South Street, a baroque fantasy overlooking the sea toward Cuba. As a kid I had played around here, swimming out and diving for conchs that I'd bring back and clean on the street, giving the shells to the black guys who would then polish and sell them to tourists visiting the southernmost point in the continental U.S. The conch meat I took home and gave to Captain Billy, who made steak from it, and occasionally conch fritters. It was an art that Phyllis never learned and had no particular interest in, dealing with those slimy creatures.

As kids we made up stories about the spooky house that sat on the corner, shuttered and half-hidden behind a tangle of palms and tropical foliage. No one ever seemed to go in or out of the place, and I can remember we would scare the daylights out of ourselves, letting our imaginations run wild.

I was shown into the sitting room by a young lady in jeans and a man's shirt, her Irish accent echoing throughout the halls.

I stood when Portia Villani came into the room on the

scent of talcum powder and brandy. In her presence I felt my youth. Portia Villani was ninety-one years old, her mind clear and sharp as cut glass. She had a strong face, an expression of puzzled merriment, I thought. I was perhaps more aware of the makeup than I might have been on a younger woman. She had gray hair piled on top of her head, loosely but deliberately covering the obvious thin patches. We had met on occasion over the years at one or two overlapping social functions, but we didn't really know each other. There was something regal and mysterious about her. Captain Billy had always ridiculed the Villanis as pretentious. My mother, I'm sure, would have disagreed.

"I have a glass of brandy at one each day," Portia said. "Will you join me?" She carried in one manicured hand a small brandy snifter and a lace handkerchief.

"Not today."

"Anything?"

The Irish girl lingered in the doorway.

"No, thanks."

The girl left, closing the double doors behind her.

Portia sat in a brocade chair with a small table beside it where she placed her brandy glass. I sat back down on the sofa facing an empty fireplace. The shutters on the windows were closed and it was dim in here, cool and slightly musty.

"I'm happy you'll be able to play," Portia said.

"My pleasure."

"There will be a band there, but I thought it would be a good idea to divide the evening so that we get a diversity of entertainment. I've never heard you play, but I'm told you're very good."

"I like the old standards. Jazz and popular. Will you be there?"

Portia took a sip of brandy. "No, at my age the crowd's too much for me."

I nodded in sympathy. Crowds were too much for me, too, and this woman was already more than thirty years old when I was born.

"Now let me see," Portia continued. "Which Lowry family do you belong to? Is your brother the senator?"

"Yes. Carl. My father was Captain Billy Lowry. He ran a charter boat in the fifties."

"Ah, yes," Portia replied knowingly. "I remember your mother then, Phyllis."

So they did know one another. Somehow I was not surprised. And knowing my father's temper and his political connection with the Bayards, not surprised that my mother would have kept it a secret.

"I didn't know her well, but I liked her. A good woman and an outsider. Like me." She took another sip of brandy.

"Mrs. Villani, I'm looking into a murder that happened in 1955."

"Oh, yes, you're also a detective, I hear. Is that why you wanted to see me?"

"I hoped you might be able to help me. A girl by the name of Lila Murphy was killed that year. They never found the person who did it."

Portia used her lace handkerchief to dab at her eyes beneath her glasses.

"Lila Murphy . . . Well, yes, I remember. She was quite young, wasn't she?"

"Just out of high school."

Portia was silent for a moment, staring into space. "That was also the year my husband was fighting Bayard Cement."

"I don't recall. I was in Korea then."

"Major portions of the highway into the Keys were scheduled to be rebuilt about that time, and the state awarded Bayard the contract."

"I'm not surprised. Bayard had the only cement company outside of Miami."

"My husband thought the work should have gone out to bid. One of those Miami companies might have been able to do it cheaper."

Vincente Villani. When had he died? More than ten years ago, I believe. And a son who was also dead. The remaining children were two daughters, who lived in this house with their mother, rumored to be recluses. Longevity definitely favored the female side of the Villani family.

"The Bayards had too many political bases covered," I said. "And still do."

Portia nodded sadly. "But Lila Murphy, I'm afraid I don't remember anything that might be of help to you." She finished her brandy, shifting slightly in her chair. She seemed tired.

I stood and apologized for overstaying.

"Not at all," she said. She stood, too, and walked with me to the door, which opened for us as we approached, the Irish girl smiling on the other side of the threshold. "I'm glad of the company. If I can help in any other way, please call."

"And if anything comes to mind about Lila, I hope you'll call me."

"I promise," Portia said.

I went out the front door and down the cobbled walk to the sidewalk where I turned and looked back, all those childhood ghost stories dissolving in front of my eyes. The mysteries, however, remained.

20

I protested the construction of a motel where a perfectly good if somewhat weed-grown parking lot had been. The kids were going to have to find some other neighborhood to score their drugs, and on the days when I was hung over and sat at my kitchen table staring out the window, instead of a mutable canvas I was now going to have to stare at the back wall of $100-a-night motel rooms. Where was their conscience?

The city commission had none. They voted 4 to 1 in favor of construction. This was a rare commission because two of its board members were Conchs. My own people, who had made something of a comeback in the last election. Apparently, they had never met a building they didn't like.

After my protest, I spent the early evening prowling the island on my bicycle, avoiding home—given my mood—and the temptations that lurked there. I went by Casey's. She wasn't home. She had saved me from myself on Sunday, but I couldn't expect her to do that every day.

I pedaled by the cemetery. Whatever temptations lurked here, alcohol wasn't going to be part of them. The gates were still open and I rode in, taking the familiar narrow paved paths with their street markers, past the green sailor who surveyed the dead from his pedestal above the Spanish-American War victims who had died on the battleship *Maine,* to my parents' plot. The Lowry plot.

From a nearby African orchid tree I had plucked some of the purple blossoms that Phyllis had favored. She was always gathering the wildflowers that grew in such profusion on the island, which those of us born here seemed to take for granted. The idea of leaving baskets of plastic flowers around the gravesites, as so many of my fellow Conchs did, always amused her. I suspect that habit had to do with the same lack of enthusiasm my people showed for the old Conch houses. There was something in our spirit that desperately wanted out of here, wanted to join with that homogenization on the mainland. Plastic flowers were the last symbol of flight from this island that bound us.

I filled the bronze vase with water from a spigot at the sextant's office and arranged the orchids. Captain Billy would scoff at such nonsense. I could hear him, that rich Conch accent, laughing: "The dead are dead. What do they care about flowers?"

Such an odd coupling, those two, I thought, standing back and looking up at the sky as it took on its evening crimson glow. There was some wildness in Billy that must have appealed to my mother, and some gentleness in her that met an unarticulated need in him. And over the years, it must have grated on both of them that they could be so controlled by the opposites in their nature.

I wondered if Carl ever pondered his parents' life together. We certainly never talked about it. In many ways I was much more like my father than I would have liked: the obsessive nature, the aggressive temperament, even to a degree the provincial mind-set. My people and I were one. Carl had, in his own way, escaped by going to Tallahassee. But despite his ambition, which may have been no more than a desire to get away from here, I thought of him as relatively passive, more like Phyllis.

And yet he'd been molded by Captain Billy in a way I hadn't been. I saw through my father's bullying, his pettiness, even though some of it had rubbed off on me, in a way that Carl had never understood; Billy had dominated him, too.

The Bayards were a good example. Carl doted on them, took them seriously, saw them as a means of escape, his salvation maybe, because Billy had worked that idea into him. I resisted it. Didn't trust it then, when we were kids, don't trust it now. The Bayards might be my people, but they were phony.

John T. Bayard was a spellbinding orator, had a gift for the gab, as they say. He could stand up there and pound a podium with the best of them, convince you that whatever he was proposing, he had only your interests at heart. He was leading this county into the twentieth century, the claim being that in those postwar years we were still living in the nineteenth.

Billy was a believer; Carl was a believer. Along with the majority of voters who kept John in office until he died in the early part of the 1970s, an old man who'd brought us closer to the twenty-first century than he ever probably imagined possible, and in so doing had crippled most of his people with a tax burden they had no means of bearing. John died a wealthy man, very wealthy, and the wealth remained in his family.

As far as I know, Carl had never benefited materially by his association with John. Carl was comfortable, but he wasn't rich that I knew about. However, he was still pushing his mentor's policies, ones that were driving this county closer to the brink. Soon we'd all be gone and the only people who lived here would be the rich, who could afford to come and spend two or three months in the winter and abandon the place the rest of the year.

One of the cemetery caretakers came driving through in his car, making the rounds, closing the gates for the night.

"Bud," the caretaker said, out his car window, "you're going to get your fill of this place one day. You don't want to spend the night now, do you?"

I laughed and climbed on my bicycle, took another turn around the town, then went home for the night.

21

The next morning I was back in the library. It was Mary Russell's day off. An assistant helped me find the fiche for the *Key West Citizen* for the first three months of 1955. I carried them to a viewer. It took the better part of the morning to read those old papers, which was like looking into a scrapbook. I went through the pages slowly, reading everything—the obituaries, the classifieds, even the ads. Steak was fifty-nine cents a pound. The Casa Marina was offering single rooms for six dollars a night. It all brought back memories. Some of these papers Phyllis had sent me in Korea.

I was trying to find information about the business of repaving U.S. 1. Little was made of the apparent conflict Portia Villani had mentioned the other day about putting the contract out for bid. That type of investigative journalism didn't make it into a small-town newspaper like the *Citizen* in those days. Especially not where a local man like John T. Bayard was concerned. If John didn't have a financial interest in the *Citizen,* he was sure to have had a close personal friendship with the managing editor. There would be no criticism of Bayard Cement.

There was mention that the whole process was being debated in Tallahassee. I decided to look at an edition of the *Miami Herald* for the same date. There I found a small paragraph toward the end of the article that suggested there was some controversy over the way the contract had been awarded. Little detail. Apparently John's tentacles reached to the *Herald* as well.

It was afternoon when I drove the Buick, still belching blue smoke, up the Keys to Rockland, site of Bayard Cement.

Buy Bayard by the Yard was painted on all the cement-mixing trucks traveling the highway, and on the huge sign on the roof of the building as I pulled into the central office.

I hadn't made an appointment, hoping to surprise Jack, assuming of course that his brother Peter hadn't already told him that I'd been around asking questions about Lila Murphy.

It was one o'clock. Jack still wasn't back from lunch, one of the women in the office told me. I didn't leave my name, just said I'd stop back later, and walked out to the quarry pit in back where the marl was dug up and turned into sand.

A line of mixing trucks was filling up at a chute and being weighed. They reminded me of elephants the way they trundled slowly in a line from one process to another, nose to tail, rumbling and leaving trails of gray liquid dripping from their big slow-spinning bellies.

The vast expanse of marl and sand piles that had been gouged from the earth was like a barren mountain range. It was a desolate landscape, all in the name of progress, paving and building where before there was only raw nature.

The whole scene was depressing, sending my mood into depths as gray as the cement that leaked from the trucks. I tried to tell myself that it was just an enterprise, as hapless as any other, but it didn't work. Even though it was irrational, I despised the Bayards and everything they stood for.

"Bud, what the hell brings you out here?"

I was startled from my reverie by Jack, who suddenly came up beside me. He wore khakis and a short-sleeved blue shirt, the collar of a white T-shirt showing at his neck. He had on steel-toed boots and a hard hat on his head. He was the picture of rough-hewn strength and health. The suburban Marlboro Man.

"Just wanted to see where the paving of paradise started," I said.

Jack chuckled. "Hey, it's an evil business. But somebody's got to do it."

"Yeah," I said, and no further comment seemed needed.

"They said in the office you were looking for me. You want to go inside?"

We walked beside each other and I felt old and out of shape beside Jack. We went into his office, the desk piled with papers and blueprints in some kind of organized chaos.

"Peter called the other day, said you'd dropped in on him."

"I thought he might."

"So what's up?" Jack was unlike Peter in every way, as different from his brother as I am from Carl.

"Trying to tie up some loose ends. I was looking through some old newspapers this morning. You remember back when they were rebuilding the highway here?"

"The new bridges?"

"No, before that. In the winter of '55."

"Oh, hell, barely. I was just out of school then."

"Weren't you working here at the time?"

"I suppose I was. I worked here every summer. Pissed the hell out of me, too, I remember that."

"I didn't know whether you'd gone away to college or anything."

"A couple years business school in Miama." The Conch pronunciation of the city 150 miles to the north.

I nodded. "There was some controversy over that highway project."

"What was that?"

"The state awarded it to a construction firm without putting it out to bid."

Jack took a toothpick from his pocket and began cleaning his teeth, sucking his gums. "Shit, Bud. I don't know what you're talkin' about."

"Well, your father was in the Senate and Carl was his aide. John T. held quite a bit of influence in the state."

"What the hell is this, Bud? You digging into something happened a long time ago. I'm supposed to remember that?"

"It's just the timing I'm interested in."

"What d'you mean, the timing?"

"A woman by the name of Lila Murphy was killed around that time, shortly before that contract was awarded."

"Yeah, Peter mentioned you were asking about her. Look, Bud, you trying to make a connection?"

"No—"

"Because anybody else, their ass would be out the door by now. I'm trying to give you the benefit, Bud. We go back. You know that."

"I know it."

"Then what's your point?"

"You remember Lila?"

"Damn right I remember her."

"Were you at that dance the night she disappeared?"

"Yeah, I was there."

"How well did you know Lila?"

"Not well enough."

"What's that mean?"

"Shit, Bud. Where the hell were you?"

"Korea."

"Right. Well, she had every kid in school creamin' his jeans over her. And none of us were gettin' any."

"Why not?"

"Because she liked older guys. Wouldn't have anything to do with anybody her own age."

"How much older?"

"Hell, I don't know. Guys in their thirties. The ones who had a life."

"You know who she went out with?"

"No. A lot of different guys. Maybe nobody special. I think she just mostly hung out. Probably a cocktease."

"You want to give it some thought? Maybe you'll remember something later."

"No, I don't, Bud. That's ancient history. We got to keep goin' forward, not backward."

I shook my head. "Only some of us. Only some of us."

22

"That was quite a speech the other night, Bud." The mayor grinned and winked. My people. We were standing in the garden at the home of the state attorney, Ray

Welch, who was hosting one of several parties he gave each year. The usual sociopolitical mix. I was here at Alex Farquar's behest and because I thought I might be able to connect with some of Key West's past movers and shakers who I'd been unable to corral earlier. At a gathering like this it was like bobbing for apples. They were all in the tub; it was just getting a grip on them.

"You want a motel in your backyard?" I felt the gentle pressure of Casey's fingers massage my biceps. At least I'd been able to talk her into coming. Hopefully, I could stay away from the punch bowl.

"Bud, the town's not like the old days," the mayor said. "You're trying to hang on to the past. Why don't you get yourself a place to live off Duval Street and just use that as an office?"

"Why don't you lower my taxes?"

The mayor laughed. He was a youngster. I used to watch him play baseball when he was a kid. Not a bad second baseman, he had good speed and knew how to play the sacrifice. "Believe me," he said. "I wish it was that easy."

"Let me guess who's behind the construction. The Bayards." As I said it, I saw Peter Bayard walk across my line of sight heading toward the bar, his wife, Evelyn, beside him.

The mayor laughed again, clapped me on the back, and moved on.

"What was that all about?" Casey asked.

"They want to build a motel fifty feet from my back door." We stood at the edge of a deck beside a swimming pool, really just a long, narrow lap pool, its underwater light casting a green tint over the area. Pathways covered with pea rock and bordered by areca palms, all lit from hidden lights, meandered through the grounds. French doors opened onto the pool deck from the house where the bar had been set up in the modern kitchen. "You want a drink?" I asked Casey.

"What are you having?"

"Club soda."

She smiled. "Me, too. Go easy on the ice."

I was halfway to the bar when Ray Welch stopped me. "Bud, glad you could make it. I hear you're working on an old case."

"Asking some questions."

"Getting any answers?"

Ray was a Bayard boy. Part of the machine. He'd been reelected for the past two terms. And it was widely perceived that he wasn't a particularly innovative state attorney, but an effective administrator of the status quo. In other words, whatever the Bayards thought appropriate was what Ray Welch brought to the job.

"Just more questions." I didn't think it in my best interest to drop any pearls into the state attorney's lap.

Ray nodded and moved on. I went on to the bar. A bartender in a tux shirt with bow tie and cummerbund was mixing drinks. "A couple of club sodas," I said. "Easy on the ice." He poured the drinks without expression and I carried them back to Casey, who was talking to Alex Farquar. He had replaced the rumpled suit with jeans, oiled boat shoes, and a fancy tropical shirt worn outside his jeans.

I glanced at Alex's left ring finger. There was no telltale band. I put my own free hand around Casey's shoulder. She gave me a quizzical look, unaccustomed as she was to any proprietary gestures on my part.

"Gideon," Alex said. "You got my message then?"

"About Barlow?"

Farquar nodded. "You were right. He's flown the coop."

"On the run?"

"That's what I think, Gideon, he doesn't want to get involved. The drug dealers we busted in Operation Cleansweep were penny-ante, just a fluke. In the wrong-place-at-the-wrong-time kind of deal. Without Barlow's testimony, they walk. But if we get Barlow lined up, I think we've got a chance at cracking the case at the very top. The dealers will talk before they'll go to jail. We need Barlow."

"You might want to look at it another way," I said.

"How's that?"

I saw Webb Conners, standing on the other side of the pool, motion to me. The whole courthouse crowd was here.

"Barlow may be up to his neck in drugs himself. He's afraid if he testifies, his own scam may come out."

"There's no record on him."

"Around here that could mean he's just lucky, not necessarily innocent." I disengaged from Casey. "I'll be right back," I said, and walked over to Webb. Out of uniform he seemed somewhat smaller.

"Bud, everybody's talkin' about the Lila Murphy case. You'd think it happened yesterday."

"What are they saying?"

"That you're out to ruin Frank Paine."

"How can I do that? Frank's dead."

"Well, you know what I mean. Frank's a legend and some are sayin' you're carryin' a vendetta."

I stared at Webb. It was enough to back him down.

"I shouldn't even be talkin' about this to you, Bud, but I retire this year and we've always been friends."

"Appreciate it. Any other information you've got I hope you'll get in touch." I emphasized *other*. We weren't going to talk about any vendettas.

"Sure, Bud. Be careful." Famous last words. Peggy's last words.

I turned to go back to Casey, but I didn't see her. It would have been easy now just to go into the kitchen and ask the kid in the tux shirt to hammer me with the rum. Forget the ice. Vendetta. I was a weak man; a man who could be thrown into turmoil and ruination by words.

Vendetta. Was it? Until now I'd never let it cross my mind, at least not on a conscious level. Phyllis and Frank Paine. Yes, they had gone out together after Captain Billy's death. Too soon after for some. Including me. There was talk that Phyllis had been seeing Frank before my father shot himself; and inevitably, that it was the reason for his suicide. Captain Billy was well loved; my mother was always the outsider.

Frank, of course, would be blameless in all this. Never married, with a reputation as a womanizer, he was free to pursue whatever sport came his way.

I never talked to my mother about it, and whatever relationship she had with Frank Paine, it didn't last. As far as I know, she lived the last twenty years of her life in a state of seclusion and celibacy.

"Bud, we meet again."

I was shocked out of my reverie by Peter Bayard, still with his wife, Evelyn.

"Tell me something," I said. "You design the new motel that's going to be built between Duval and Simonton Street?"

"As a matter of fact, yes."

"I thought so." What I'd conceived of as an eyesore had now in my mind become grotesque. Perhaps, as the mayor suggested, it was time to think of moving.

"Jack said you were out at the plant."

"Yeah, we had an interesting visit. I'm trying to remember, you had established your practice here in 1955, hadn't you?"

"Yes. Why?"

"And you and Evelyn were married then?"

Evelyn looked at me curiously. "We were married in 1954," she said. She had been a glossy blonde. She was a few years younger than Peter. Always very stylish, very aware of her good looks and the money that kept them that way.

"What are you getting at?" Peter asked, an edge creeping into his voice.

"I was curious. Jack told me that Lila Murphy was into older men, guys who'd established themselves. I just thought—"

"Who's Lila Murphy?" Evelyn asked.

Apparently there was one person in town who didn't know what I was doing.

"I'll tell you," Peter said, taking his wife by the arm.

"Did you say you didn't dance with Lila that night?" I asked Peter before they could leave.

Evelyn looked up at her husband with some irritation. I had sown some family discord. It seemed the least I could do for a man who was going to ruin my view for the rest of my life.

I was at the bar holding out my empty cup about to ask for rum when Casey came over. "Hi, sailor," she said. "Long time no see."

"Did he get your number?"

"Who?"

"The slick lawyer."

Casey laughed. "Jealous?"

"Maybe. You didn't answer the question."

"He asked. I didn't give."

"Let's celebrate."

"My place, or yours?"

"Yours," I said. "There are fewer ghosts."

23

On my way home from Casey's the next morning I stopped at the drugstore for breakfast and sat down at the counter on the stool beside Sweetwater. He glanced up. "Bud," he said, then went back to eating his eggs, mixing them together with the grits on his plate. The knuckles on his large hands were well-defined, and the veins crisscrossed like roadways on a map. Sweetwater pushed the food onto his fork with Cuban bread, carrying it to his mouth in a backhanded grip. He was a model of passive indifference, a man who had seen everything there was to see on this island but chose not to comment. Sweetwater was one of the men whom I'd given conchs to when I fished them from the sea near the Villani mansion as a kid.

"The usual," I said to the waitress when she brought my coffee.

I was beginning to feel better, a night of love and several days without a drink, almost whole again. My cure.

"Sweets, you remember Frank Paine?"

"Who gonna forget him." Sweetwater had a deep well of a voice, soft but modulated. Phyllis used to walk with Carl and me in the summer to the black church not far from our home on evenings when Sweets would be singing in the choir there. You could hear his bass voice booming more than three blocks away.

"Seems to me Frank had someone from black town

working for him at one time," I said. "You know who I mean?"

"Titus."

"That's him. Titus Walker. Is he still alive?"

"Was last night. No reason to think he is this mornin'. He in bad shape."

Titus Walker had been Frank Paine's right-hand man for a few years. He was still around when I returned from Korea, something uncommon in those years, to have a black man in a position of authority in a small Southern town like Key West. But Frank Paine had always marched to a different drummer, and Key West after all had supported the Union cause during the Civil War, though mostly because federal troops were here, not out of loyalty to the Union.

"I'd like to talk to him," I said.

" 'Bout Frank?"

"Yes."

"I hear you rakin' up the past."

"Looking into an old murder case."

"I hope you remember what the Bible says."

"What's that?"

" 'Vengeance be mine sayeth the Lord.' "

"And is that what you say, Sweets?"

"I say you best be careful. You may find yourself diggin' up what best be left buried."

Advice it seemed I was getting from all quarters.

Sweetwater had more coffee while I finished my breakfast. Then we drove over to Mickens Lane in Sweets' old Dodge pickup, a relic of the era I'd been thrown back into with its straw-and-horsehair stuffing poking out of the seats, the floorboards rusted out, and the hood ornament—a flying horse, its chrome chipped and one wing missing—pointing the way.

Titus Walker lived in a shack on a weed-strewn lot.

Tar paper covered the framing studs where the siding had rotted away or was missing. A black mongrel with open sores on its haunches crawled out from under the house and limped toward us, its sides heaving and tongue hanging out its mouth.

"Tights," Sweetwater called as we approached the house. "Gotta visitor."

I followed Sweetwater up two loose cinder-block steps and across the doorless threshold into a small kitchen where the simple plumbing was exposed, no cupboards, a piece of plywood for a countertop that held several near-empty pint bottles of Seagram's whiskey.

"Tights," Sweetwater called again.

The rest of the house was unfinished and contained only a few sticks of furniture; the floor plywood, the walls old, exposed two-by-four studs, the rafters holding the peaked roof, its tin barely visible, mantled with cobwebs.

Titus shuffled into view, apparently from the bathroom. He wore bedroom slippers and shiny black pants held up by suspenders, and a dirty old-fashioned undershirt. His eyes were rheumy and his hair the color of piss holes in powdered snow—an old man alone, sick, dependent on others.

" 'Member Bud Lowry?" Sweets asked.

Titus nodded in my direction and pointed into the kitchen. Sweetwater went and got him one of the pint bottles from the plywood counter. Titus took a swig without offering it. My own eyes watered.

"Bud want to talk to you," Sweets said.

Titus put the bottle in his baggy pants, turned, and walked into the shell of his living room. There was a daybed with sheets the color of his hair where Titus sat down, a wooden kitchen chair next to it stacked with old papers, and Titus motioned to it. I moved the papers onto the floor and sat down there, less than a couple of feet from Titus, the smell overpowering.

" 'Member your daddy, Bud." Titus spoke barely above a whisper, his voice slow like it was being strained through mud.

I smiled. Everyone remembered Captain Billy. Sweets had even been in the marching band that played at his funeral. "I wanted to ask you about Frank Paine," I said.

For a moment some life came into Titus's eyes.

"You remember Lila Murphy?" I asked.

Titus shook his head.

"The girl killed up by the bat tower in '55."

"Oh, yeah." Titus reached in his pocket for the bottle and killed it in one swallow.

"You were working for Frank then, weren't you?"

"For ten years."

"Frank had that investigation shut down. You know why?"

Titus shrugged. "No evidence, I guess."

"They didn't even do an autopsy on that girl."

Titus motioned to Sweetwater, who brought him another bottle. "Frank always had his reasons for what he done. He didn't always tell 'em to me."

"But you were right there, his right-hand man. You might have seen something—"

"Might, but didn't. Bud, I can see you got your daddy's eyes. Don't be tryin' to look with them where you can't see. Do you no good." Titus sank back onto the bed and sucked on the bottle.

Sweets put his hand on my shoulder. That was all I was going to get from Titus Walker. A man who had held this community together when others were being torn apart with race riots. Frank had known what he was doing when he hired Titus. And Titus would protect him right to his grave.

24

Peggy was making bread. The only woman I ever knew, including Phyllis, who still baked bread. The kitchen smelled of yeast and flour dust.

"Bud, sit in the other room," Peggy said, handing me a cup of coffee. "I've got the oven on and it's going to get too hot in here."

I carried the coffee into the living room. The difference between this life and Titus Walker's was painfully obvious—day and night. Night and day. Be still my heart. Where did I belong? Probably in neither.

The piano I had left with Peggy when our marriage ended was up against the far wall. She had told me that Barbara was taking lessons. A couple of molded busts of Mozart and Bach were on the lid of the upright, a lesson book open on the rack. A thin wedge of sunlight spread across the shag carpet, dust motes suspended in the light.

"Bud, sit down, for heaven's sake. You look so awkward standing there."

I sat down on the piano bench facing the living room and balanced the mug of coffee on my knee. I prefer kitchens. They serve a definite purpose and seem to me easier to negotiate than rooms like this. Peggy sat on the couch.

"I just came from Titus Walker's over on Mickens Lane."

"Titus?"

"He worked for Frank Paine."

"Oh." Peggy took a sip of coffee, and I could see a patina of flour still on her fingers. "Jake told me you've got a feud going with the Bayards."

Peggy's husband worked for the Florida Keys Aqueduct. The people who brought us our water 150 miles through a pipe from the mainland. Our lifeline. The navy had installed the pipeline in the fifties, later turning it over to the civilian authority to operate.

"Peggy, they want to build a motel in my backyard."

"That's what the Bayards do, Bud. Build things."

"I'd just as soon not have to look at it every day. Peter's a lousy architect."

"You can't fight them, Bud. Besides, they're your people."

I laughed. "I was thinking about that the other day. The Captain used to say the same thing."

"Well, they did a lot for your family. Where would Carl have been without John T.?"

"What about Frank Paine?"

"What about him?"

"He was John T.'s man, too, wasn't he?"

"Oh, Bud." An exasperated tone of voice. "This is a small town. We look out for our people. Like any other small town."

"Even when our people are corrupt."

"You mean Frank? Frank wasn't corrupt."

"How do you know?"

Peggy hesitated. "Well, I just know. Everybody loved Frank."

"Every woman he could get his hands on, you mean."

Peggy teased a curl of hair back into place. "Bud, what's the point of this?"

"You know his reputation."

"He wasn't the only man in town with that reputation." She glared at me and I saw the humor in her eyes, which had once shown fire, and remembered the arguments we had had when I would come in late after a gig.

I took a drink of coffee. "Phyllis." I could utter my mother's name, but even to Peggy I could not put the question that would couple her with Frank Paine. But Peggy knew. I saw the recognition in a simple sideways glance that was as common to her as the color of her eyes, and betrayed any evasiveness.

"Bud, don't."

Peggy and Phyllis had been close, more like mother and daughter than in-laws, even before we were married. Peggy hung out in the house on William Street when we were in high school. And when I went to Korea, Phyllis never failed to mention Peggy in her letters.

"You know the rumor. Was there truth to it?"

Peggy shook her head. "What's the point of this?" she demanded. "What are you trying to do to yourself?"

I wasn't sure. I didn't feel any anger over a betrayal of Captain Billy. So maybe I had simply invested too much virtue in Phyllis and had trouble admitting her shortcomings. Seeing her toppled from her pedestal was in a sense recognition of my own failure as a son. In my lack of ambition I know I must have been a disappointment to my mother.

"Just tell me," I said to Peggy.

She looked me in the eyes; her expression seemed frightened, like she was unsure of my reaction. "Yes," she said.

Well, now I knew. Nothing was changed. It was a long-ago transgression that today would have meant nothing. Nothing. Now I knew.

"While I was in Korea?"

"Yes," Peggy repeated.

"How long did it go on?"

"I don't know. A year maybe. It was over when you got back, I know that. Although I think they may have gone out briefly after your father died, before Frank moved to Ocala."

"Did she ever talk to you about it?"

Peggy shook her head. "Only once she said that she hoped you and I would get married and have kids. And that I never had to go through what she was going through."

"What did she mean?"

"I don't know. I didn't ask her and she didn't say anything more. It was about this time of year and I remember we were in the kitchen in the house on William Street. We had been talking about you."

"Where was the Captain?"

"I don't know. Fishing probably."

"And Carl?"

"God, Bud, I can't remember that. I suppose he was in Tallahassee."

"Did either one of them know about Frank Paine?"

Peggy shrugged. "You know how rumors are in this town."

Yes, I knew. I couldn't have been back from Korea more than a few weeks before some wag at the Garden of Palms got drunk one night and popped off his mouth. There was a fight, and from then on no one mentioned Frank Paine and Phyllis in the same breath. At least not in front of me.

I wondered if my father had ever had an encounter like that. I tried to remember any significant details of their marriage during that time, but nothing came to mind. They argued, as they always had, but a few months after returning I moved into my own place. And not long after that Peggy and I were married.

So what did Phyllis mean? Hoping Peggy never had

to go through the same thing. And why was I dragging all this out now? What was the point of this? as Peggy asked. Was it just a score I had to settle? Nothing to do with Frank Paine and Lila Murphy. Perhaps all of them were right. Drop it. Do not look where your eyes can't see.

25

Back at the office I stood at the wall and studied the photographs of Phyllis and Captain Billy side by side in their individual frames. My mother and father; their faces stared back at me from the sepia tones of wartime. Phyllis was somber, a dark-eyed beauty, her expression suggesting, at least to me, some inner disturbance. Captain Billy was grinning, playful, maybe even clowning for someone—Phyllis?—on the other side of the camera. Of the two my father's expression was the more familiar. I remembered him in this attitude more than any other. Phyllis had always been unpredictable. There was also a graduation picture of Carl from a later time—a handsome, studious-looking young man. I would have been in junior high school. My family. The memories that came back. I was no longer sure I knew them anymore.

Frank Paine. Sweetwater. Titus Walker. The Bayard and Villani families. Back then, they were all in their prime, active in their own ways in the community. Lila Murphy, too, was alive. How many times had I seen her on the streets or in school?

I sat down at my desk and scrawled their names on a piece of paper. Beginning with Frank and Phyllis. Captain Billy was left dangling, along with Lila Murphy. Carl belonged to the Bayards, Sweetwater with Titus, and the Villani family to Key West. At least on my list, despite the fact that they weren't umteenth generation Conch.

I picked up the phone and called George Lewis at the police station.

"The Lila Murphy murder," I said when he answered.

"You're still beating that horse." George laughed. "It won't run."

"After the dance, the police interrogated everyone who'd been there."

"That's the standard procedure. So?"

"I wonder if those records are still around?"

"You kidding? That was back in the ice age."

"But it was an unsolved homicide. When did you start throwing the paperwork out on cold cases?"

"When the paper rotted."

"You're sure?" I persisted.

Lewis sighed. "Bud, you can be a real pain in the ass."

"But you'll take a look, won't you?"

"I'll take a look," he growled. "When I get a chance."

"You're my people," I said, and hung up before he could dispute it.

I went to the kitchen and made a sandwich from cold cuts, lathering the bread heavily with mayo, and then stood eating it over the kitchen sink while casting glances now and then at the lot out back where the Buick was parked. There was no sign of the Bayard construction team in there yet. But it was just a matter of time.

The phone rang as I was rinsing the crumbs down the sink. It was Alex Farquar.

"Gideon, how would you like to get off the rock?"

The rock being the island, the place that anchored me like a ball and chain. I couldn't remember the last time

I was out of the county, these hundred plus miles of islands that dissolved into the mainland.

"Barlow?" I asked.

"The very same." I could picture Farquar in his office, his sleeves rolled up, the phone cradled against his shoulder while he pawed through file folders of other cases. Unfortunately, I could also picture him leering at Casey.

"Tell me," I said.

"We believe he's in New Orleans."

The city of dreams. I had never been there.

"So have him picked up," I said.

"It's more delicate than that. Legally time consuming, and time I no longer have. I've got a court date in a couple of weeks. Operation Cleansweep."

"So what can I do?"

"Go out and talk to him. Lend some of your gentle persuasion to get him back here."

"How gentle?"

"He's got to come back voluntarily."

It seemed futile. I remembered the house on Cudjoe Key, abandoned in a hurry by a man whom I could not see anxious to return.

"He's going to want a baby-sitter," I said.

"That would be you. Once you get him here we can turn him over to the state's witness protection services."

I thought it unlikely, but said nothing. The SA's office wanted to pay my way off the rock for a few day's leave, who was I to argue. It may have been just what the doctor ordered. A way out of the consuming obsession I had developed with the past. Today was Tuesday. I had until Friday night before I was due back at the Club. I told Farquar I would leave today. He gave me what particulars he had on Barlow, and I called and made reservations for a flight to New Orleans. I would be there by early evening. Then I called Casey at the graphics business and asked her if she would feed Tom for me. I would leave a key for her in the bromeliad planter by the back door.

"Just when I was getting used to you again," she said. "Are you running away from me?"

"No. If I could work you into the expenses, I would take you with. Watch out for Farquar."

"Watch out for your own damn self and mind your manners in New Orleans."

Loosely interpreted, I understood it to mean stay away from the bottle. I packed a small bag, then drove the Electra to the airport and boarded the next flight out to Miami.

26

Nothing about New Orleans reminded me of Key West. Except the tourists. I got a hotel off Canal Street, outside the Quarter. It was raining and cold. In a dime store on Canal I bought a long plastic slicker that came rolled up in a packet with a rain hat, saving the receipt for Alex Farquar.

It was early evening when I walked across to the Quarter and found a large restaurant that had a counter where several men my age sat alone and ate. I bought a copy of the *Times-Picayune,* went in, and ordered gumbo soup and codfish pie. Me, oh my.

Kenneth Barlow had a sister living here. Her address was on a slip of paper tucked in my billfold. I dug it out. Appropriately, the place was on Elysian Fields. And no doubt a streetcar named Desire would take me there, but I decided to rely upon a taxi.

I asked the driver to cruise slowly past the house, go a couple blocks, turn around, and come back and park three houses away from Barlow's sister's. Then I sat back and watched the rain and the meter tick over, waiting to see who might come in or leave the house. I ran the gamut of conversation with the cabbie about life in Florida. Which of course wasn't life in the Keys.

I was a home boy and I began to realize, sitting there staring out at this foreign world, how insulated I'd allowed my life to become. As the world was reduced in size by every space shuttle that lifted off from Cape Canaveral, I drew more inward. I sought less; I expected less. At one time there might have been something to learn by getting out from under the shell that we Conchs carry on our backs, but with satellites recording every atmospheric change, every tribal movement in Africa, the biggest mystery left is: Who am I? I can remember when hurricanes used to sweep out of the ocean and strike with the suddenness of lightning. Now, we're tracking them as they form off the coast of Africa, like babies, watching them, a blob of color on a TV screen, advance hour by hour westward.

There are no surprises anymore except in the way that we surprise ourselves.

I saw a light come on in the window of the house I was watching. The cabbie was smoking one cigarette after the other, filling the car with a dull, constricting odor and fogging the windows. He was talking about basketball.

I opened the door and felt the rain-freshened air invade the cab. "Hang around," I told the cabbie. "I'll be right back."

Shaped eucalyptus trees grew along the curbside. I

walked down the sidewalk to the modest bungalow, a white frame job with a curtained picture window. I pushed the buzzer on the porch and listened to it chime inside. I heard footsteps, and a woman opened the door.

She looked to be in her mid-twenties, and something in her demeanor reminded me of Casey. A kind of innocent curiosity that hadn't been deadened by fear of strangers. I smiled. "My name's Gideon Lowry. I'm with the state attorney's office in Key West, Florida."

Her expression didn't change noticeably. "About Kenneth?"

I said it was. She pushed open the door and invited me in.

"My name's Karen."

I entered the living room with its low, encrusted ceiling that reminded me of the beginning formations of stalactites in the entrance to a cave. A light suspended from the center of the ceiling from a gold chain gave off a paltry yellow glow, giving the shopping-mall furniture a look of cheapness it probably didn't deserve. More stucco covered the walls, the one behind the couch holding two framed paintings on cloth of brightly colored roosters. Macramé held pots of sphagnum moss from which twining, waxy leaves cascaded. In the center of the floor was a child's playpen filled with toys. I shuddered as I tried to imagine living in such an environment. Even Peggy had not been reduced to this.

"It's a mess," Karen said, as if that were the problem. "I just put the kids to bed."

"How many?"

"Two. A boy and a girl."

Karen was attractive in a bland sort of way that seemed to match her surroundings. She seemed innocent, sweet, totally without guile.

There was no sign of a male influence here and I assumed she was raising the kids alone. I stood awkwardly beside the playpen as Karen went through a brief—thankfully—summary of her day with the kids. Mentally, I retreated to the back of the cab with the smoke and the cabbie's blather of the NBA play-offs.

"Coffee?"

"What?"

"Do you want some coffee?"

"No, thanks. About Kenneth—" I began.

"How bad is the trouble he's in?"

"I don't know, but I would like to talk to him."

"He isn't here."

"But you know where he is?"

She glanced down at the synthetic carpet. When she looked back up, there were tears in her eyes. "He's my only brother and he's been good to me and the kids." Karen looked around the room, surveying the contents.

"I understand."

"I'm divorced. Without Ken I'm not sure what we'd do."

"I'd like to talk to him. I can't promise anything, but I'll let him know where he stands."

Karen nodded, wiped at her nose with a handkerchief she took from her pocket.

"Will you ask him to get in touch with me?"

"Yes, but I can't promise anything either. He's scared."

"I know that." I dug beneath my raincoat for a pen and a scrap of paper in my shirt pocket. I wrote my name and hotel down, along with my room number. "I'll be here until Friday," I said, handing her the paper.

Karen clutched the paper in her fist. "I'll tell him."

I left, walking back across the sodden ground to the waiting cab, and a more familiar world. By changing geography, I had escaped temporarily the ruins of my own family, only to replace it with the ruins of another. The rain had slackened to little more than a heavy mist, but the cold was in my bones. I sought sanctuary in the Quarter, along with the other nameless tourists, and found a bar where another man's blues came out of a horn.

27

I was testing myself, something I had done a hundred times, telling myself each time that I could do it. Have a couple of drinks and walk away. There were times when I'd been successful, but for each one of the successes there had been ten failures. Tonight though was going to be different; I knew it.

I sipped the first drink slowly, savoring it while I listened to the dirgelike rendition of the black trumpeter's "St. James Infirmary." The place was dark, seedy, fitting my mood, which had been watered down by the weather and Karen Barlow, or whatever her last name was.

Karen was the victim of circumstance, and given her condition, worthy of some pity, but she was young and strong and she would find a way to survive. Someone else to take care of her. Her brother, it seemed to me, was a different matter. Without even meeting Kenneth I had formed an image of him that I was sure wouldn't be too far off the mark. I had seen it so many times in the Keys. When a young man would come there looking for adventure, make some easy money in the drug trade, then decide he could finance a lifestyle. Barlow had done it and then, to validate himself, began supporting his sister. He could have done worse things. But now he was in over his head and scared.

I wasn't quite so sure that Barlow would contact me, but I thought there was a good chance Karen would talk him into it. Whatever he did, I didn't really care. I had already made up my mind how I was going to handle him, and if he didn't show up, I would just go back to Key West. Farquar would have to prosecute his case without Kenneth Barlow.

I was forty-five minutes nursing one drink, some kind of record, and when the trumpeter took a break, I found a pay phone hanging on a graffiti-covered wall. I dialed Casey and listened to the phone ring seven times before hanging up. It was an hour later in Key West, after ten o'clock there. I had no holds on her, no reason to expect her to be at home, but I felt a keen sadness when she wasn't.

I decided against another drink and walked out and down the rain-darkened sidewalks. The rain was forgotten now except for the drip from overhanging balconies and cars splashing water from their whining tires. The Quarter was bathed in neon light, which gave a blue quality to the night and seemed to reactivate the streets after the rain. Two women in tight dresses overtook me, their voices deep baritone and bitchy. There was something retrograde about the Quarter that reminded me of the fleshpots I had visited when in Korea.

I walked back to the hotel, gave a dollar to a black man missing a leg who stood on crutches in the debris that had collected in the entrance to an awninged grocery store closed for the night.

There were no messages at the desk. I went up to my room, took off the rain slicker and laid it across the dead radiator, then stretched out on the bed. The walls were covered in old-fashioned wallpaper and I stared at them, letting my eyes trace the design, picking out the rhythm of the patterns. Half an hour went by. I got up, turned the TV on, and picked up the second half of a basketball game, one of the play-off games my cabbie had been talking about earlier. The Bulls and the Knicks. With the volume off I watched the play with the same sort of interest I'd had in studying the wallpaper.

Just before eleven the game ended, and without knowing who won I watched the flickering images of a commercial as I put a call through to Casey in Key West. Again seven rings, and I hung up. I shut the TV off and walked over to the window and stared down at the denizens of darkness, who were out now like earthworms after the rain.

I don't remember Phyllis or Captain Billy ever traveling farther than Miami. As much as we wanted to imitate life on the mainland, for the most part my people were not good travelers. Maybe some inward fear that if we got too far from the home front, it would be taken from us. In our temperament arrogance and insecurity competed for dominance.

I wanted to go home. I felt old, and used up, while irrational thoughts of death crept over me. The idea of dying alone in a hotel room in a city of strangers, the way Virginia Murphy had, depressed me further. I thought of calling Carl in Tallahassee but decided he would only accuse me of being drunk. Instead, I went to bed. And lay there sleepless, guarding against the demons, until sometime in the early hours of morning I fell into a dreamless sleep.

When I woke, the sun was shining through the gauze curtains covering the windows, and the phone was ringing. When I picked it up, there was a click at the other end.

28

The next day, Thursday, slithered by with the indolence of a mirage along a slow desert crossing. I had a four-o'clock flight back to Miami and spent the better part of the morning lounging around my room after being granted a two-hour extension to the one-o'clock check-out time. I wanted to give Kenneth Barlow every opportunity to make contact. By noon I decided he wasn't coming and went down to the café next to the hotel and ate a sandwich. I thought about calling Karen, but I had told her when I was leaving New Orleans so it seemed pointless to remind her. Either he was coming or he wasn't. And frankly, Scarlett, I didn't give a damn.

The phone rang when I was back in my room a little after one. I answered it, expecting to hear the desk clerk checking to see if I still wanted the extension. A voice not the desk clerk's said, "This is Kenneth Barlow."

"Glad you could make it. I was getting ready to leave."

"Can I come up?"

"If you hurry." I heard the phone drop into its cradle, and before I had time to finish taking a leak there was a knock at the door. When I opened it, Barlow, looking pale and shaken, stepped inside.

He was just what I'd expected, thirty-odd years old, still wearing his youth like bad skin that wouldn't go away. He had blond hair that was trimmed close around the ears, long and unruly on top. He wore expensive sneakers, a T-shirt with a bloodred heart painted into the palm of a hand, and jeans. When I closed the door and turned around, he was standing at the window. On the back of his T-shirt was the name Jim Dine.

"Expecting someone?" I asked.

Kenneth shrugged, stepping away from the window. His young face seemed startled, the area beneath his eyes as gray and tight as sharkskin, and I guessed he probably hadn't slept in several days. I wondered what he was on.

"Karen trusted you, man. Otherwise I wouldn't be here."

"Believe me, I wouldn't be here either, Ken, if the Monroe County state attorney's office wasn't paying me."

"To bring me back."

"That's what they want."

"What are they offering?"

I relayed Alex Farquar's offer of protection.

"And how good's that?" Barlow asked.

"It's got a pretty good success rate as long as you play by their rules."

"And what are they?" He sat down on the edge of the bed.

"Sealing your life off for a while. Going underground."

Kenneth studied his shoes. I let him think. "What if they don't get a conviction?"

"You're still covered."

"Shit, man, I've got a house there."

"I know. I've been in it. You forgot to lock the doors when you left."

"What's gonna happen to it?"

"It can be sold, no problem. Maybe take a loss but you pocket the money."

"And live like I was in fuckin' jail."

I didn't say anything, it wasn't my place, at least until I was asked. Which somehow I knew I was going to be.

Barlow stared up at me plaintively. "What would you do?"

I paused, but I didn't have to think about it because I'd already done my thinking. Kenneth Barlow was a pawn, a witness to a crime in which he'd played some marginal role. Farquar wanted to bring him back to put pressure on the kingpins in the state attorney's investigation. In Key West, Barlow's life wouldn't have been worth a plug nickel, no matter who was protecting him. "If I were you, I'd take off. Go out to California, Hawaii, anyplace like that and start over. You're young. Why put yourself through this?"

"Straight?" He continued to look at me, but his expression had changed. He looked scared. Shit, I thought, it isn't what he wanted to hear. He wants to be taken in, someone to take care of him. But I didn't want to be that someone.

"Straight," I said.

He rocked forward, putting his face in his hands, his elbows on his knees. "What about Karen?" he mumbled.

"She'll be all right. Better off with you on the run than worrying about you while you wait around Key West to testify."

Barlow sat for a moment motionless. Then he bucked up, throwing a fist into the air. "Goddamn it! How did I get into this mess?"

I didn't say anything, waited. He got up and walked to the window. "Why are you doing this? You're supposed to be bringing me in."

I felt like a father with a wayward son, but I didn't tell him that. Nor did I tell him that I didn't want the responsibility of baby-sitting someone who had all the earmarks of being a cokehead. "I don't know," I said. "It just seems like the right thing to do."

Barlow turned back from the window. We looked at

each other. He was trying to hide his fear. "So all I do is walk out of here, right? And everything will be okay."

"Ken, get into a new line of work. Go sell insurance or something. You're not cut out for this."

He came past me, and for a moment I thought he was going to shake my hand, but he was trying to regain a macho posture as if I were rejecting him in some way. He was out the door before I thought to say good luck.

I walked to the window, parted the curtains, and watched him leave the hotel. Saw him walk across the street, almost jaunty as if he were beginning to feel his freedom, when a car seemed to come out of nowhere at speed. I saw Barlow pause, turning as he stepped onto the sidewalk, and for an instant he was blocked from view. When the car passed, Kenneth Barlow lay on the sidewalk, blood spreading across the Jim Dine heart on his T-shirt.

A crowd had gathered around Barlow by the time I got downstairs. Someone had called an ambulance, the distant scream of a siren cutting the air. I made a space through the crowd and gazed down on Barlow's gray face. There was nothing anyone could do for him anymore. He was dead. No doubt about that. He'd been shot through the heart, I guessed at least twice, though it was difficult to tell with all the blood. I went back to my room.

I dialed Karen's number, heard her voice when she picked up the phone on the second ring, then listened to myself as though I were someone else explaining what had happened to her brother. She held up until the end, asking questions as she tried to understand what could have happened.

It was quite clear. I had made it easy for whoever wanted to kill Kenneth Barlow. Rather than hunting him down themselves, they had simply followed me to

New Orleans and waited for me to do the legwork, not realizing that Barlow had been no threat to them. Also thanks to me, because I had talked him out of it. But it was a thankless piece of business all around. Had I walked out with Barlow, I had little doubt that we both would have been gunned down.

I caught my flight to Miami and the commuter to Key West. At nine o'clock that night I was back in the Club playing "Someone to Watch Over Me."

29

Monday morning the Bayard trucks rolled into the parking lot out back. *Buy Bayard by the Yard.* The notices had gone up while I was in New Orleans, and I had had to hunt for another off-street parking spot for the Buick, which turned out to be a block away from home. By the time I went down to the courthouse to find Alex Farquar, my mood was as jagged as the rip of the jackhammers tearing up the former parking lot.

"Who knew I was going to New Orleans looking for Barlow?" I demanded when there was a recess and I got Farquar alone in a hallway.

"Easy, Gideon. What happened?"

"Barlow was killed, that's what happened. Shot down on the street like a dog as soon as he contacted me."

Alex shook his head in a manner that annoyed me. Anything he did would have annoyed me. "Other than Ray Welch, I don't think anyone but me knew you'd be out there. Why?"

I restrained myself from asking him if he was stupid.

"Because it leaked out I was going after Barlow, and ten to one whoever killed him was linked to the guys you're prosecuting."

Farquar got a hurt expression on his youthful face. Annoying me further. "Gideon, I can't believe it."

"Believe it. And you better do some serious thinking because I want to know where that leak came from."

I turned and walked away. Trying to get control, I went down to Yesterday's for a cup of coffee. Webb Conners was there on his midmorning break. I joined him at the counter.

"Bud, you're back."

"Who said I was gone?"

"That's what I heard around the courthouse."

"Yeah, you hear the time and place of my last crap, too?"

"Something eating you, Bud?"

"Sorry, Webb. It's been a rough few days."

"Talk about it?"

"I lost a witness."

"How'd it happen?"

"He was shot leaving my hotel."

"Oh, boy!"

"Probably because of too much talk around the courthouse."

"I'm sorry, Bud. But you can't keep this town from talking."

"Except when they don't want to talk, then you can't start them."

"Your brother's in town. Have you seen him?"

"No." It was not unusual for Carl to arrive here without announcing himself. There were times when he would come into town and leave without calling. I never took it personally. It was just Carl's way. I finished my coffee and got up to leave.

"Bud," Webb said, "I guess you wouldn't have heard about Titus Walker."

"What about him?"

"He died while you were away."

I studied the tile floor. Sweetwater had said that Titus was on his last legs. Now another voice was silenced, another coffin going in the ground at the cemetery, and another nail in the lid of Frank Paine's legacy. "I talked to him the other day," I said.

"I heard."

Of course. "Old age and the bottle?"

Webb nodded. "The whole enchilada."

"I guess that leaves you the senior man from the Paine administration."

"Bud, why don't you leave that go? It's a dead-ender."

"Maybe. But I don't think so. I believe we all know things we think we don't know. It's just we got to find a way to access it, isn't that what the computer boys call it?"

"And maybe we want to forget it."

"I'm not going to let that happen." I left a dollar on the counter and walked out.

Something about leaving here, spending those three days in a foreign city that might just as well have been a foreign country as far as I was concerned, returning to find my own familiar territory in upheaval, had renewed my dedication to Virginia Murphy. Only now it wasn't Virginia I was working for so much as myself. I hadn't even deposited that check. There were things now I wanted to know, would know, because it was a matter of preservation. I walked up the street, my shirt sticking to me in the May air heavy with humidity, and jangled the ship's bell that hung outside Carl's Key West office. This had definitely become a family affair, and it was time to air out the closet.

30

As a boy Carl was sickly. It seemed that Phyllis was constantly taking care of him. I remember a long bout of rheumatic fever along with the normal childhood illnesses of measles, mumps, and chicken pox—all of which seemed to take a greater toll on Carl than on other kids. When he was well, Phyllis pampered him. I never remember Carl diving for conch in the sea around the Villani mansion, or exploring in the backcountry, where my friends and I practically lived during the long hot summers, getting there on the small outboard-powered skiffs we had. Carl was definitely coddled. My vivid memory of Carl is of him lying around on a bed in the screened-in back porch, reading when I would come in from a day of play. And what surprises me on thinking back about it is not the attention Phyllis gave him but the sympathy Captain Billy had for the invalid.

Carl had a weakened heart as a result of the rheumatic fever. He spent his entire life on medication. His bathroom and kitchen held a pharmacopoeia of prescription bottles and vials. He walked with a slight limp and had a delicate look, but in his adult years he had not suffered the long periods of debilitating illness that had laid him low as a kid.

Women were drawn to Carl, but he had never let himself get attached—for reasons that I could only guess at. Although I'd once entertained the idea that he might be gay, now I think he was just too afraid of the complications of marriage as a result of the domestic troubles he'd seen between Phyllis and Captain Billy, or maybe because of his health he had somewhere along the line concluded that he was not a good candidate for a husband. But it was always maybe. I just never knew because Carl never talked about it. At least not to me.

The truth is Carl and I had never been close. We inhabited two different worlds, so much so that even as kids I had a hard time seeing him as my brother. He was studious and moody, a mama's boy, and I was keenly aware of having to compete with him for her attention. Since she was always fostering his intellect with books, I suppose it was only natural that I also developed an interest in reading. In one area I had one definite advantage over Carl in Phyllis's eyes. I was musical; he was not. Getting me to practice the piano was another thing, but Phyllis must have recognized the talent in my playing that was absent in Carl's.

As for Captain Billy, I think he must have foreseen that Carl's talents lay in a broader, more significant range where the Lowry name would gain some lasting recognition beyond that of someone pounding a keyboard in a Key West nightclub. Which is why he could tolerate Carl's early sickly years. It would certainly explain Captain Billy's forbearance of Phyllis's constant mothering, and Carl's sissified upbringing. As well as their apparent relief when Carl left home, seemingly fit and under the wing of the Bayards. When Carl left, it was almost as if I were cast loose, too, even though I was still in high school. It seemed like they were done with parenting. Captain Billy began carousing. And Phyllis, too, it appeared, had busted loose in her own way.

Climbing up the steps to the porch of the Conch house where Carl had an office with a small apartment above it, I thought about these things. It also struck me how much we had in common. Both of us living in Conch houses, miniaturized beside what we'd grown up in, our offices a part of our domestic life as if neither one of us could get away from the distraction of our work. Also, there was the irony of geography. Carl's place was no more than a block from John T. Bayard's old homestead where Peter Bayard now lived, while I was a couple of blocks from the Villani mansion, which I suppose reflected our differences as clearly as anything either one of us could have said.

I rang the bell again before turning the handle and stepping into the reception area where a secretary who worked for Carl part-time was at her desk, cradling a telephone to her shoulder as she pecked away at a computer terminal. I suspected the call was a personal one because she hung up as soon as I came in. She smiled. "Hello, Mr. Lowry." She was a Conch whom I spoke to only occasionally on the phone, but seldom saw.

"Mornin', Miss Sawyer. I hear Carl's in town."

It was cool in here, centrally air-conditioned, all the office furniture comfortable, but not so expensive Carl's constituents would feel out of place. There was Key West art on the wall, mostly pastel watercolors of Conch houses. Decorative and noncontroversial, just like Carl tried to be.

"He hasn't come down yet. Shall I call him and let him know you're here?"

"Please."

It was not yet ten o'clock and Carl, like his pal Peter, never started work before ten in the morning. I watched her pick up the phone and punch the intercom button. I heard footsteps on the floor above me, and soon after Miss Sawyer said, "Your brother's downstairs, Carl." She listened, smiled, then hung up. "You can go on up," she said to me, as if I'd been granted a special favor.

There was a door that closed off the L-shaped stairway. I opened it and went up. Carl greeted me at the top of the stairs. I don't remember when we'd last seen each other. He was taller than I am, and thinner. He had Phyllis's looks, thin-lipped with a long, slender nose that hooked downward slightly at the tip. His narrow-set blue eyes seemed paler than I remembered. We shook hands. He had on a pair of neatly pressed slacks with a white shirt, no tie, and suspenders.

"You look good, Bud." He was lying. Over his lifetime Carl had developed a skill of making ingratiating remarks, but I knew him well enough to see the truth in his eyes. I was overweight. My T-shirt was stained, my khakis crumpled, and my face was still puffy from the drinking. I hadn't shaved this morning and I wondered if I reminded Carl of Captain Billy, whom I most closely resembled.

"We need to talk."

Carl looked at his watch. "I've got an appointment at ten-thirty. I can give you half an hour."

My brother. "I'll take it."

There was something different about Carl since the last time I saw him, and for a moment I couldn't tell what it was. I followed him into the kitchen. Carl was barefoot. The kitchen was a mess. A Lowry kind of mess. Except for Phyllis none of us had been great housekeepers, and even Phyllis let go of some of that obsessiveness once most of the men were gone. But the difference between Carl and me was that Carl had a double standard—one for his outside world, another for his private domain. I worked the way I lived.

I sat down on a padded barstool next to an island counter about four feet long in the center of the tiled floor. I watched Carl wash out a couple of mugs in the stainless sink before filling them with recently brewed coffee from an expensive electric percolator.

"Let's go in the other room," Carl said, handing me one of the mugs.

I followed him down the hallway again and into his small living room: a rattan couch, a wicker princess chair with its sculpted back, and a TV in one corner. Carl made a hasty attempt to pick up magazines and scattered clothing, which he tossed into the bedroom where I could see the unmade bed. On the coffee table were the remnants of an unfinished meal. He scooped the plate up and carried it back to the kitchen. If his constituents could see him now. The only personal items were some photographs and various plaques and awards on the walls. Most of the photos were of Carl with some vaguely familiar political figures, several with him and different governors of Florida. There was even one of Carl and the President. None of Phyllis, Captain Billy, or me.

I had never visited him in Tallahassee, but I wondered if his place there was as free of remembrance of things past as was this apartment. Carl came back and sat down on the sofa, putting his bare feet up on the coffee table. His feet were narrow, shaped like Phyllis's but with little tufts of hair growing on his toes that was a Lowry inheritance.

"Someone's coming in to clean up tomorrow," Carl said as if he felt a need to explain. He took a sip of coffee. I sat down in the princess chair. "How have you been, Bud?"

"So so. How about you?"

"Can't complain." Carl had always been taciturn. Except when he was politicking. He was like a stranger to me and yet I found myself curiously attached to him in a way I'd never experienced. He was my brother, my connection with the past, and as different as we were, I felt an affection for him that probably only members of a family linked by tragedy and death could feel. Sentimental? Probably. I brushed the thought away.

"I was in New Orleans last week."

Carl looked surprised. I was not one to venture far from Key West.

I explained what had happened down there.

"It's an unpleasant business you're in," Carl said.

"Rarely unpleasant. Mostly just tedious. Even though a lot of the people I work for are unhappy, I don't think you're talking about unhappiness."

Carl shook his head. "No. Peter Bayard tells me you've been questioning him. And Jack."

For an instant I saw Phyllis in Carl's expression. The way he had of interrogating you without ever asking a question, holding your eyes while he spoke and then at the last minute examining his hands. It was Phyllis to a T.

"The Bayards are building a motel in my backyard."

"And you're harassing them because of a construction job?"

I smiled. "That's what they're calling it, harassment?"

"Bud, we're too old for this kind of thing, these petty differences."

"You going to tell me that the Bayards are my people, the way Dad used to."

Carl looked perplexed, as if he'd forgotten Captain Billy's favorite expression. "You've always had a thing against the Bayards. I never understood it. I still don't."

I chuckled. Mr. Chuckles. "Well, call it principles, a commodity that's in short supply among the Bayards."

"Bud, where do you come up with this stuff, this"—Carl seemed to search for a word—"this moral superiority. Principles! What do you know about their principles?"

"I know that John T. fixed it so that Bayard Cement got the contract to repair the highway back in the midfifties."

For a moment Carl seemed caught off guard. His toes twitched on the coffee table. "You have an obsession with ancient history."

"It's history. Our past. Not so ancient. Somewhere along the line I heard we were supposed to learn from it."

Carl groaned, a sound weighted with despair. "You'll never grow up. Going on sixty and you still carry that silly idealism around with you like a teddy bear."

I shrugged. Who was I to argue?

"Things have to get done," Carl said weakly.

I didn't reply. It was strange to see him here like this. Big brother. And I realized now what it was that was different about him. He had lost weight. Carl had always been thin, like Phyllis. However, this was not just a fluctuation due to diet but rather a change in mass, some final transmogrification taking place, and as I looked at him, Carl reminded me of that sickly kid who had lived so much of his early life on a daybed in the Florida room of the house on William Street.

Carl looked at his watch.

Time to go. I stood up. "Let's have dinner," I said.

Carl nodded absently and picked at a fingernail. "Sure. We'll do that."

32

Listening to George Lewis's voice on my answering machine, I watched the Bayards' boys digging trenches for the footings that would be filled with cement, the foundation for the Deep Six Motel, the not inappropriate name that was being given the place, written on the sign that towered over the construction site.

Lewis said he had something for me and suggested I drop by his office at one o'clock. It was almost noon. As the construction crew began to break for lunch, I saw Clint Bayard walk over to a pickup truck and take out his lunch pail. I left the house and walked down the worn path to my former parking lot. Clint was sitting by himself on the ground eating a sandwich, his back against a palm tree.

As I approached, he grinned at me without speaking and continued chewing. Clint was the runt of the litter. Peter got the Bayard looks and a certain style to go with them, while Jack bore the stalwart strength of the clan. It was his strength, I think, that drew my brother, Carl, to Jack as they got older. Clint, left on the short end of the gene pool, had staggered through life from one fuck-up to another. But somehow the Bayards had managed to keep him out of serious trouble.

"I've been trying to remember," I said, standing over Clint so that he had to look up at me, squinting against the sun, "how many years I've been looking at this empty lot. What took you guys so long to come around and ruin my view?"

Clint lifted a hand helplessly. "Hell if I know, Bud. Stuff changes."

"Too bad it doesn't change for the better."

Clint ignored that—or maybe he didn't get it. His arms and shoulders protruding from his T-shirt were thin and bony, the flesh slack, and there was a roundness to his shoulders and his belly, not the paunch of a middle-aged man, but more the distension that comes from slackness. He was probably about Casey's age, early forties, born late in his father's life. John T. had in fact died when Clint was a young man.

"You running the job?" I asked.

"Looks that way. Until they find something better for me to do."

"Well, I'd like you to do something for me."

"What's that?"

"Put up a fence between me and your construction here. Spare me some of the noise, the dirt, and the sight of this thing."

"Hey, Bud, I don't know about that. I don't think we're budgeted for any preconstruction fences."

I smiled. "What I'd like you to do is go to Jack and tell him that Gideon Lowry wants a fence up between his house and the construction area. Tell him that, Clint."

Clint shrugged.

"And if he doesn't agree, tell him I'm going to be over here every day watching this thing, examining every code restriction, making sure you follow the letter of the law. Which may be something new to the Bayards. The first violation I find I'm going to get this job red-tagged and then fight your asses through the state courts if I have to. It might just be easier to put up the fucking fence."

A small crowd of construction workers had gathered

around, sensing perhaps some hostility and not wanting to miss out on something that would provide them with conversation when the day was done and they were in the bar throwing back some cold ones.

Clint stood up. Although I didn't think he was going to pursue this further, Clint was always a wild card. I rolled my shoulders a couple times and flexed my ancient knees. Even with the fifteen additional years I had on him, I was pretty sure I could take him.

"You threatening us?"

"Call it what you will, but get the word to Jack."

Clint glared at me and I held his eyes. There was a murmur among the laborers. Finally Clint said, "Get the fuck outta here. I got a job to do."

I grinned and saluted. Turning, I couldn't resist a little grandstanding. I winked at the crowd, then walked back to the house. I guessed that there would be a fence up by this time tomorrow. If there wasn't, I had every intention of making good on my threat.

33

I felt a certain keen edge, a kind of excitement that I had forgotten existed when battle lines were drawn. An adrenaline rush maybe, but there was something to be said for drawing lines in the sand as I had done with Bayard Cement. It heightened my sense of being, although I knew full well its bittersweet companion, futility.

So my thoughts ran as I made my way to the drugstore

for lunch. On the way in I ran into Sweetwater, who was just going out.

"Sorry to hear about Titus," I said. "I was out of town."

Sweets nodded. "He be better off. Glad you got to see him, Bud. Tights a good man got knocked down by the bottle."

Sweetwater's face held no other expression than the one I'd seen there for the forty-plus years I'd known him, so I didn't take his remark as an admonishment. I watched him walk down the sidewalk to his pickup before going in and sitting down at the counter and ordering a bowl of red bean soup.

After lunch I ambled downtown to George Lewis's office. George had his feet propped on the desk and was throwing darts into a dart board on the opposite wall.

"Anyone in particular?" I asked, aiming a thumb at the dart board.

"I don't name names. It just settles the gastric juices after lunch."

George was wearing his customary guayabera, a four-pocketed shirt with ribbing, favored by the Cubans. Even though he was not a big man, the shirt was stretched taut across his ample belly. The striking feature about George Lewis was his uncommonly small hands and feet. There was a delicacy about him, the way he held the darts he threw. I sat down at the desk opposite him and waited while he plunked the remaining darts into the pockmarked wedge of the number twenty. When he was done, he removed his feet from the desk and picked up a manila file.

"You got lucky," George said.

"The dance?"

George nodded. "When they found Lila Murphy's

body up behind the bat tower, the sheriff had jurisdiction."

"Frank Paine."

"Right. Up until that point it had been a joint investigation between the county and the city. I found this in some old files buried in the basement." He handed me the folder.

I opened it and found several photocopied sheets of official reports, some typed, others handwritten. "You look through it?"

"A glance. Nothing unusual. A preliminary inquiry. But it has the reports on everyone who was at that dance."

"Any problem if I take it home?"

George shrugged. "Hey, the original's back in the file."

"You're a prince among men."

George laughed. "Don't get carried away. I'm putting it in the debit column. You owe me one."

"How are the wolfhounds doing on the most recent Murphy case?"

George formed a circle with his thumb and index finger. "We're about ready to chalk it up as an accidental death."

I stood up.

"Bud, I'd just as soon not have this come back on me. Whatever use you make of that"—he pointed to the folder on the desk—"you didn't get it from me."

"Understood." I picked up the folder. "Take it easy, George."

He got up and walked me to the door, taking his darts from the board on the way. "You still on the wagon?"

A crazy expression I'd never understood. I was neither on nor off the wagon but rather in some riderless wasteland absent any choice in the matter. I felt as if I'd been stripped of free will, simply moving along on automatic that had nothing to do with what I wanted or didn't want. I wondered where Casey was, why I hadn't heard from her since I got back.

I left George Lewis standing perplexed in the doorway, with his darts clutched in his hand, and wandered over to the courthouse.

Judge Watson was expected back from lunch at any minute although he was not due in court this afternoon, according to his secretary, who invited me to sit in the waiting room if I cared.

I thanked her, took a seat, and went through the folder. Names, names, names. Most of them I knew. Some, like Hal Westerby, the Bayards, I'd talked to. I puzzled over the police notes, the hurried responses to questions, looking for something, anything that might provide a clue, another starting point. I noticed that those of prominence, like the Bayards, were hardly questioned at all. And like Carl Lowry.

My brother, Carl. It never occurred to me that Carl would have been there because I'd associated him for so long with Tallahassee. But there his name was among the stellar list of local bigwigs. At least we'd have something to talk about at dinner tonight.

34

Sweat stains showed beneath the arms of Judge Watson's seersucker suit as I followed him into his chambers and we sat down at the conference table in front of his desk. Phyllis had always referred to him as Justice even before he was on the bench, and eventually that had become abbreviated to Just. I would have to think to come up with his birth name.

The judge set fire to the tip of a cigar from a kitchen match that he had to hunt for in all the clutter on the conference table. In the gray, dead smoke that curled up from his cigar, I framed a picture of his wife, Willa Lowry, a younger distant cousin of Captain Billy's, who married Just when I was in high school. Ten years later, pregnant, Willa died in a car accident. The loss of both his wife and unborn child changed Just Watson in a way none of us could have imagined. He withdrew into himself, never remarried, and though he occasionally attended the Lowry family gatherings, he spent most of his time alone. Speculation among the family was that he would probably never have become a judge if he hadn't lost Willa so early. As it was, he devoted himself to law, studied it, read all the great legal scholars as if in search of a way, I thought, to put the world right again. In the process he became something of a legend on the bench. Once he made circuit court judge, he never sought an appointment to a higher court, turning down all that were offered.

Just had no politics that I know of but a reputation for being incorruptible. Such are the distortions of age that though barely ten years older than I, the judge had assumed for me an almost paternalistic role in my life.

"I saw your brother the other day, Bud. He's worried about you."

I smiled. "Funny. I talked to him this morning and I'm worried about him. What's his problem?"

"Your conflict with the Bayards for one."

"And a conflict with the Bayards is always a conflict with Carl."

The judge grinned, worrying the cigar deeper into the

corner of his mouth. After years of cigar smoke in here the smell was humid, slightly musky, the smoke so absorbed into the books, the papers, and the furnishings that the entire room reminded me of the cigar factories that had once been a part of Key West. Where Cuban men sat by the day rolling the damp leaves of tobacco, their fingers brown and slender as the cigars they rolled and shaped. Phyllis had taken Carl and me as kids to the small cottages around town where we watched them work. By that time the big factories had moved to Tampa, taking with them the readers who had been hired to entertain the workers, but every time I smelled a cigar I was reminded of those times.

"You want to talk about it?" Just lifted the cigar from his mouth, and a dusting of ash scattered over his seersucker suit as he reached for the ashtray.

"I just had an encounter with Clint Bayard, who seems to be the project manager at a new motel that's going up a hundred feet from my back door."

"You must be sitting on some prime property there, Bud. The way that end of Duval Street is building up you could probably make a few bucks if you sold."

"That's what the mayor suggested the other night at Ray Welch's do."

"Well—"

"Driven out by the Bayards."

"More the times, I would say."

"So where do we take a stand?"

"Ah, Bud. Isn't it a little late in the day for taking that kind of a stand? Sell, and buy someplace where you'll be comfortable."

"I'm comfortable where I am."

"Doesn't sound like it."

"Well, I told Clint to put up a fence. They can do that

or fight me through the courts. You know as well as I do the Bayards are going to be cutting corners every chance they get."

Just nodded and drew on his cigar, one eye closing against the smoke. "Carl also mentioned you'd been questioning the Bayards about an old murder case."

"That's right. The Murphy girl who was found up around the bat tower in '55."

"You ruffling their feathers?" Just chuckled.

"I might be. But Carl of course is going to protect the Bayards all the way to their grave."

"Have you got some evidence, anything to go on?"

"All I'm doing is asking questions. I promised a woman I'd do that much."

The judge nodded again. Then for a moment I thought he'd gone to sleep. When he opened his eyes, he said, "Bud, you may have bigger problems than an old murder case and political cronyism."

"Like what?"

"Alex Farquar."

Farquar. I remembered my angry encounter with him this morning, the first since I'd returned from New Orleans, and my general disaffection for the man, which was based more on his style than anything substantive. I assumed the judge had heard about the trip to New Orleans. I was right.

"I think Farquar set you up," Just said.

"Barlow?"

"I've got to have your word that nothing I say goes outside this room."

"Of course."

"I don't have any proof. But you ought to look into it. He's stonewalling the Cleansweep case. To watch him in court you'd think Farquar worked for the defense, not the prosecution."

Barlow. I saw him crossing the street from my hotel in New Orleans, walking quickly as if he'd been suddenly freed. How did Farquar know that Barlow had a sister in New Orleans? I should have questioned that. I didn't.

"My hands are tied," Just said. "Without something to go on I can't make any claims."

Farquar had been with the SA's office a couple of years. I had worked for him maybe a dozen times. It was not the first time there had been bad apples in that office. We'd had our share of corrupt attorneys, some had even sat in the top man's chair. Farquar was young, probably underpaid, as lawyers go, frequently a compromising combination.

"I'll look into it," I said. "But you know it will be impossible to keep quiet."

Just shrugged. "Go easy. Maybe nothing will come of it." He rolled the cigar in the circle formed by his thumb and index finger. "But whatever happens, don't bring it back here."

"You know I wouldn't do that."

The judge closed his eyes again. After a moment I got up and left.

Carl was late. I was accustomed to that. He had always done things according to his own timetable with little regard for how it might inconvenience anyone else. I think Carl simply believed that what he had to do was always more important than maintaining a schedule. Although I don't think it was consciously deliberate, it had been his way of establishing his identity, growing up as he had in the shadow of illness. And it was that, I suppose, which had always made it so easy to forgive Carl.

I sat at a table in a hotel restaurant overlooking the harbor. Carl's choice. I had never been in here. When I was a kid, this land had been a boatyard. Now there was starched linen and a pleated napkin in a pale shade of pink folded in a semicircle facing me. I looked at my watch. Eight-fifteen. In the harbor beyond the window the lights on the red and green channel markers winked. A coast guard ship, its deck lighted, passed on its way in to dock. Strangers came and went, a bright-faced waitress came to take my drink order.

Barbancourt on the rocks, I told her. A squeeze of lime.

Just before eight-thirty, Carl walked in. I had seen him arrive moments earlier and watched him stand at the entrance talking with several people whom I didn't recognize. Carl was courtly, smiling. He wore a light summer suit. As he walked to the table, I was more aware than usual of his limp. He smelled of cologne, a lemony scent, expensive, that he'd favored since high school when he was learning sophistication.

"Am I late?" Carl asked without waiting for an answer. "I got held up." He sat down opposite me, his eyes sweeping over my casual attire, the half-empty drink in front of me.

The same beaming waitress came and took his order. He asked for a bottle of white wine, something French. I reflected on how little either of us had changed. We were both just complex extensions of our original selves.

Carl looked better than he had this morning. Maybe I'd caught him at a bad time. Still, when I studied him, there was a certain lifelessness about his eyes that made me think he was less well than he tried to pretend. He had such a concern about his appearance of health that if I asked him about it, I was sure he would not tell me the truth.

"How long are you here?" I asked.

"I'm speaking at the benefit next week."

I was surprised. I couldn't imagine Portia Villani asking a Bayard spokesman to appear at a Villani-sponsored event. "Did Portia Villani invite you?"

Carl laughed. "Bud, you're so out-of-date."

"Probably. And you've changed?"

"Those old-time factions don't apply anymore. We're all working for the common cause."

"Sounds good. You putting that in your speech?"

The waitress brought me another drink, which I hadn't ordered.

"It's on the gentleman at the table over there." She pointed to a table across the room. Jack Bayard waved at me. Carl had turned to look. Bayard and his wife were seated with another couple I didn't recognize. I felt like I was surrounded. In the enemy camp. But of course, according to Carl, that was the old politics. We were all one happy family now.

"You see?" Carl said. "Give up these old habits. They're reactionary."

Politics.

Carl gave the waitress his order, using a modest accent to pronounce the French cuisine.

"When were you first elected to office?" I asked when the waitress was gone.

Carl looked puzzled. "'Fifty-six, I think. Why?"

"Just curious." I was aware of Carl watching me as I took a sip of the fresh drink.

"How's your battle going with that stuff?"

"I'm winning the war." I had never discussed my

drinking with Carl. In fact, apart from Casey, I had never discussed it seriously with anyone that I could remember. Phyllis had worried about it, but she had never confronted me directly, always going through Peggy, with whom I refused to talk about it. Phyllis would have mentioned it to Carl, but I was the wayward brother, outside his ken.

"Bud, something seems to be bothering you."

"I called you a couple of weeks ago."

Carl twirled the stem of his wineglass between his thumb and forefinger.

"Why didn't you tell me you were at that dance?"

"What dance?"

"The one the Murphy girl was at just before she was killed."

"Good God, Bud! Is that what this dinner's about?"

"Carl, I'm investigating a murder."

Carl smiled thinly. "That was years ago," he whispered.

"And I've got reason to believe whoever killed her is still around."

"Didn't they finally decide it was some stranger, a drifter who showed up at the dance?"

"I thought you couldn't remember anything about that dance."

Carl's eyes narrowed, he was showing me his senatorial look. "Bud, why are you giving me the third degree?"

"Because you, among others of our town's society, were at that dance, and nobody bothered to question you."

"I don't like the tone of this, Bud. Of course we were questioned. Frank Paine questioned us."

"If so, it was perfunctory. It never made it into the record. Neither you nor the Bayards. Maybe others."

"Perhaps because there was nothing to go into the record." Carl's sarcasm edged out his anger.

"And perhaps there was and Frank Paine was covering it up."

Carl brushed the air with his hand. "What nonsense."

"Did you know that Phyllis was having an affair with Frank?"

Carl looked stricken. I was reminded again of his weakened physical state. "Malicious gossip!" he hissed. He looked around at the Bayard table as if help were there, as it always had been.

I shook my head. "Someday, I have always seen the two of us sitting on a porch in this town reminiscing about the old days."

Carl tried to surreptitiously take a pill he'd dug from his pocket. I could almost hear his heart fibrillating.

"But maybe neither one of us could stand it," I said. "Too much has been swept under the carpet."

"Why are you doing this?"

"Maybe it sounds pretentious, but I'm trying to get at the truth, right an old wrong." I watched Carl's elegant fingers toy with the wineglass.

When our food came, we ate in silence, but even that was loaded, and when we separated soon after ten o'clock, it was clear that we were each glad to be on our way. Alone once again.

36

I rode around the town, a little drunk, heady with family turmoil and aware that I would be unable to sleep now.

I absorbed the night smells, drank in the feverish energy of another summer night that was as threatening as an approaching storm, or impending sex. I rode by Casey's. There were no lights on, nothing to indicate if she was home. It was after ten and I chose not to stop. Aimlessly, I kept riding, replaying the evening with Carl, while being overcome with a pervasive feeling of guilt.

Had I pushed him too far? Our worlds were estranged enough as it was. Except for our past we had so little in common. Carl was aging; *a tattered coat upon a stick,* the line of some poem came to my mind. I wondered what Captain Billy would have made of us now. Carl alone and frail, and like me, afraid of the past. What right did I have to push him along streets he had no interest in walking?

Carl, the one bright hope of the Lowry family, was after all that early ambition just another aging man limping around the halls of the state capitol. The best he could hope for would be a street or a bridge to the mainland named after him. That would certainly have made Captain Billy happy.

And Phyllis? Who knows. She was a complex woman who while she was alive had successfully hidden her complexities from the men in her life, men who would never have understood them. In the last couple of weeks I had come to realize that I had never known my mother. She was a mysterious figure, as much a stranger to me as Portia Villani.

I was riding around the dimly lighted back streets, the eerie shadows of tropical foliage spreading across my path like fallen angels. The cicadas hummed. Lizards occasionally darted from one darkened leaf to another. I had no idea how much time had gone by, but I realized I was only three blocks from Casey's, and that I'd been riding in circles.

I rode back down her street, and as I did, a car turned at the next intersection, its headlights briefly stabbing me half a block away. It slowed as we passed and I glanced back, saw it stop in front of Casey's, the lights extinguished. I turned at the intersection, rode a few feet, then came back to the corner and stopped.

I watched Casey get out of the car, a man holding the door for her. They walked up the sidewalk together to her house. I turned around and went back down the street, heading home. The man with Casey was Alex Farquar.

At home there was a bottle of Barbancourt in the cupboard above the kitchen sink, and I lifted it out and poured a couple fingers of the amber nectar into a glass, which I carried outside. I sat on the back step and looked across at rudiments of new construction. No fence had gone up. Several forms had been built, awaiting concrete that would no doubt be poured tomorrow.

I drank and felt the night grow ragged around the edges. In New Orleans, just a couple nights ago, it had been raining when I had tried on different occasions to reach Casey by phone. The world was as stable as a twisted noodle. I went back inside and poured more Barbancourt, said to hell with it, and carried the bottle with me back outside. The phone rang and I said to hell with that, and to hell with some other things, too.

The Bayards and their construction, for one. Alex Farquar for another.

Tom came out and lay beside me on the porch step, staring into the night, his paws expanding and contracting against the wooden step. I stroked the back of his ears and he purred gratefully.

I don't know how long we sat there. At some point Tom rose up, his back arched, and he hissed. The foundation forms began to take on the shape of squat dogs, pugnacious monsters guarding the new world. I could practically hear them growl, taunting me as their wooden feet dug into the ground. Tom hissed back at them, then retreated.

I slipped trying to stand up, banged my leg against the edge of the porch, and swore. I needed a weapon, something to fend off the rabid dogs in case they decided to encroach. I found it in a drawer in the kitchen. A fourteen-ounce claw hammer.

When I went back outside, the hounds from hell began to yammer steadily, and I knew I was going to have to take the battle to them or risk being overpowered later when I was asleep.

I stepped toward them, could see their lips curl over bared teeth, the growling low and insistent, waiting. I moved in, took a swipe at the lead dog, catching him in the chest with the hammer, and felt him buckle. The rest were easy. I took them out one at a time, felling them with a couple of blows of the hammer, then toppling them into their own shallow graves.

I had gone through the pack, then was going back to finish off the wounded when someone grabbed my arms from behind me. "Bud, what the hell do you think you're doing?"

I dropped the bloody hammer. I didn't recognize the voice.

"Who's it?"

"Doug Bailey."

Bailey, a night security guard.

"Jesus Christ, Bud. I didn't know it was you. I was coming back from a coffee break, I saw someone ripping hell out of the place, and I called the cops. It's three o'clock in the morning, Bud. If I'd known it was you, I wouldn't have called them, but—"

Bailey had loosened his grip and I knelt down on the

ground, saw the lights of a cruiser flashing on the side street, the cops' flashlights jabbing the dark as they walked toward us.

Doug Bailey said, "He's over here. It's Bud Lowry. I think he's drunk."

Indeed.

37

It was not the first time I'd been in jail. When I returned from Korea, there was a readjustment associated with the changes in my world, and some indiscretions: fights, youthful pranks that landed me and my friends, or combatants—often one and the same—in the hoosegow for the night. But that was prior to my career as a cop. Now it was simple embarrassment coupled with a hangover that made any confrontation painful.

Webb Conners and Early Summers stopped by my cell the following morning when they came into work. They grinned and wisecracked. The story was all over town. Gideon Lowry was sabotaging Bayard Cement. Tearing it down as fast as the Bayards could put it up.

I didn't have to say anything about the condition I'd been in—my appearance said it all. "When am I getting out of here?"

Webb's laugh grated on my nerves. "About five years. Judge Watson's throwing the book at you."

"Ah, Webb, can't you see he's suffering?" Early said. "They're releasing you on your own recognizance, Bud. You'll be out before noon."

"Any charges?"

Webb shook his head. "Jack says he isn't going to press charges as long as you don't cause them any more trouble."

I was out by eleven. I went home and unplugged the phone and began the tedious chore of nursing myself back to health. I could hear the construction going on out back, the forms being rebuilt, but I didn't bother to look outside. I wasn't ready to revisit the battleground. No one came by, for which I was grateful. Sooner or later I would have to confront people, but I didn't want to do it today.

The next day the local paper carried the story on page two of the crime report, with the headline "Lowry Tilts at Windmills." With the phone plugged back in I began answering calls. There were many, most of them distant relatives and old friends I hadn't seen in a while. They were all jocular, good-natured calls, and I took the ribbing in stride. There was no call from Casey. And none from Carl. Carl, whose sensibilities I'm sure I had offended at dinner and aggravated further by this latest escapade, I could understand. Casey was another matter.

I was surprised when Portia Villani called and sympathized. She took the incident seriously, seeing my antics as a political act, some form of civil disobedience that she supported. I didn't tell her I had been drunk as the proverbial skunk and hallucinating at the time. And when she invited me around at one for her own daily ration of brandy, I accepted.

Just Watson called, amusement in his voice as he repeated what Early Summers had already told me about the legal situation as it pertained to the Bayards.

George Lewis called, wondering why I hadn't invited him along for that drink we were supposed to have, which might have saved me some trouble.

All in all this was destined to be one of those historic events in Key West, never to be forgotten, told and retold, embellished upon until the story had a life of its own, with little regard for the truth. The night Gideon Lowry tore down a motel in his backyard. For the next few weeks I would be unable to venture out of the house without being reminded of it.

I poured whatever rum I could find down the sink and took the pledge. Once again. Although I had tried and failed on my own, I was unwilling to admit that I lacked the will, the power, to do it myself. Stubbornness was a trait that ran deep in this family. We believed in our ability to control our individual destinies. And we didn't let our problems outside the family. Just look at Captain Billy, who put a gun to his head before admitting powerlessness—his way of keeping control. And Phyllis. The outsider whose self-abnegation in the face of Carl's chronic illness was simply a way of hiding from the misery of her marriage. Now Carl himself, even at this age, was unwilling to confront the flaws, the personal peccadilloes, of this family.

It was not surprising that Casey would find it difficult to relate to this private obstinacy, she who had recognized her own failure and depended now on public recognition to save her.

I didn't blame her for her unwillingness to participate in my failure, but in light of what had happened in New Orleans and Just Watson's admission, her association with Alex Farquar was troubling. I had always accepted her other relationships due to our age difference and my own questionable suitability. In the past I'd never known whom she went out with. But not Farquar. Was it because of him that she was keeping her distance?

At noon, I shaved, then for the first time took a look out the back door. A fence had gone up. And the hump of one of Bayard's cement trucks was visible over the top of the fence. The cement was being poured, the foundation solidified. The Bayards had won. To the victor belong the spoils.

At one o'clock I rode my bike over to the Villani mansion.

38

Irish, her red hair tied back with a green band across the top of her head, showed me once more into the baronial room where I'd last met with Portia Villani. Irish offered me a drink, which I declined, then left me to wait the brief interlude until the grande dame made her appearance.

Portia had said she would contact me if she remembered anything about the Murphy case I was working on, and I hoped that was why I was here. But I also wanted to ask her about Phyllis. Phyllis, whose life was suddenly shrouded in mystery. Some part of me wanted to leave that mystery buried while another waged a war to unravel the whole thing. One thing I knew: I wasn't going to turn this into town gossip. Whatever inquiries I made had to be discreet, among people I trusted. Just Watson was one, and, I thought, Portia Villani.

She came in bearing her tumbler of brandy, and the lace handkerchief, her step steady, her eyes pale, almost colorless, but lively. I was standing by the empty fireplace, leaning against the mantel.

"Well, Gideon," she said, putting the drink down on

the table, its surface gray with water spots. "You've had some adventures since you were here last."

"Some I could have done without."

"I'm sure. But we're not always given a choice in these things, are we?"

My admiration for this woman skied. She seemed to command a framework that was held together by a moral center, yet her tone was neither patronizing nor demanding. Her ancient features had lent her face an oriental cast, an expression of quizzical amusement, grounded but apparently open to discussion.

"Any more than we're given a choice in the matter of our parents," I said.

Portia nodded and sipped her brandy. "I take it you are still foraging around in the past."

"The Murphy murder, yes."

"I've been doing some of that myself. Going through my husband's papers. He kept all kinds of documents and written records. I thought there might be something from that time to help you." She paused.

"I appreciate your taking the trouble."

"It wasn't trouble. It's"—she seemed to search for a word—"refreshing. At my age so much of life after all is just stored memory. I enjoyed it."

"You must have found something."

"Well, I don't know for sure, but I wanted you to see it. The last time you were here I mentioned that Vincente had been fighting the Bayards over the highway reconstruction."

"The one that didn't go out for bids."

Portia nodded. "Did you look into that?"

"I confronted Jack Bayard about it. He was ready to throw me out of his office."

"After this latest incident I'm surprised he's even speaking to you."

"I'm sure he won't be."

"Is he taking you to court?"

"No. Not as long as I keep my distance."

Portia shook her head. "Judging from my impressions of you, I doubt you'll be able to do that."

So. She had some information for me and it had to do with the Bayards and Lila Murphy. It was not unexpected. I remembered Jack's conversation at his office. His irritation with me, but also with Lila Murphy. The girl who had every boy in school creaming his jeans. *A cocktease.* Jack's words. The girl who was looking for someone older, established. Turning down boys like Jack even though his future was assured. Lila was looking for maturity and Jack Bayard didn't measure up.

But murder? Anything, I had to admit, was possible with the Bayards. They were unaccustomed to rejection. They had grown up with the sure knowledge that whatever they wanted, they could have, even if it meant bending some rules.

Maybe I was being too hard on Jack after what I'd been through with him. I wanted him to be guilty, to have someone finally put the screws to the Bayard family. And it made perfect sense that the Villani family, after their years of rivalry, should be the one to do it.

"I went back through some of my husband's diaries," Portia was saying. "He may have even discussed this with me, he probably did because he, too, was looking to stop the Bayard machine. But I don't remember it."

Portia paused and took another sip of brandy.

"Vincente picked our girls up from school every day. They went to Mary Immaculate. It was part of Vincente's schedule, something he had wanted to do."

The Villani daughters were rumored to be recluses now in the mansion. Though we must have been about the same age, I didn't know them as children because they went to Catholic school.

"It was during that highway conflict," Portia continued, "in 1954 or '55. The twins were in the last year of high school, I believe. Vincente was consumed with the way the Bayards were trampling the legal process. He was looking for any way he could find to break up some of the power they had accumulated."

A difficult task. Bayard power. It was limitless. I thought I understood it. Their hold on this county went beyond politics. It was their identification, their culture, as much inherited as the Bayard looks, and had nothing to do with anything they earned. It just came with the territory, and people like Carl bought into it.

"My husband, Vincente, saw Lila Murphy and John T. Bayard in a car together on one of the days he picked up the girls."

"Why would he make a note of that?"

"He didn't then. Not until a couple of weeks later when Lila disappeared after the dance, and her picture was in the paper."

Yes. It would have raised a question mark in the mind of someone like Vincente Villani. But of course there was no way he could confront John T., or even bring it to the attention of the authorities. Not when the authorities were Bayard people. Our people, Captain Billy said.

But with Jack Bayard's comments fresh in my mind, it now seemed to carry more weight, and I knew, as did Portia Villani, that no, I wouldn't be able to keep my distance from Jack Bayard.

39

In regard to Phyllis, I had perhaps expected too much from Portia Villani. I was looking for revelation, someone who could explain the mysteries of the universe, or at least my mother, who at one time had been my universe, but it was not to be. Portia simply had not known Phyllis well enough. I shouldn't have been surprised that Portia knew more about her foe and rival, the Bayard family, than she did about my mother, whom she regarded as a friend despite the infrequent times they saw one another. After all, we spend more time looking for flaws in our enemies than our friends.

"I remember Phyllis as being very shy," Portia said. Silent for a moment, she seemed to want to tell me some fact, something important about my mother. Finally she said, "I think what impressed me about Phyllis was her quiet determination."

Yes, quiet. Determined. That described Phyllis, but it didn't tell me enough. I wanted to know where it came from, why she was so determined, and whom, if anyone, she was guarding against.

"Your brother was ill, I believe," Portia said. "Phyllis worried about that, the effect it would have on him later in his life."

It was a partial explanation, but one I already knew.

"Do you remember Frank Paine?" I asked.

If there was any recognition of a connection between Paine and my mother, Portia didn't show it.

"The sheriff? I hadn't thought about him in years. Why do you ask?"

"He investigated the Murphy case."

"Of course. Well, Frank was connected with the Bayards as everyone was who was in a position of authority in those days. And I'm not sure it's changed much even with all the newcomers."

I nodded my agreement. After my recent conflict with the Bayards I had to agree. Portia had finished her brandy and I could see that our time was up. "I appreciate your help on this," I said.

"I hope it has been a help. It's funny, but even though it was such a stressful time, I enjoyed revisiting it."

Portia stood up, and as if on some silent cue, the doors opened and Irish came in. She helped Portia to her feet, then the three of us walked to the door.

"Good luck," Portia said when Irish opened the front door for me.

As I turned back to take Portia's hand, I caught a glimpse of a woman looking down at us from the top of the stairs. When our eyes met, she hastily retreated. One of the daughters?

"I'll keep you informed," I said, and walked down the cobbled sidewalk to the street.

After only half an hour in the dim, musty-scented house with its decades-old furnishings, I felt as if I'd been released from a time capsule. I walked down to a tourist trap for lunch, avoiding the drugstore and any remaining commentary on my conflict with Bayard Cement.

I had reason now, sufficient reason for me anyway, to pursue my investigation of the Lila Murphy murder with renewed intensity. I recognized the need to separate that ancient antipathy toward the Bayard family from the quest I was on; still, I felt some relief, some accumulated vindication perhaps, for the intuitive direction I'd been following despite the skimpy availability of facts.

Facts, like clues, had been trampled over for years. I was looking more at the characters involved, searching for a motive. That search was driving me back into myself and a family life I'd never examined until now. It had created a strain on the already tenuous relationship I had with my brother. I knew my next move could broaden that rift to an unbridgeable gap, but I would have to live with that, as I had to live with the knowledge that I might never learn the truth.

I walked home from the diner, uncertain about how to go about confronting Jack Bayard, and humbled by the burden of my ancestors. My people.

There was a message on the machine from Peggy asking me to call her back. She answered on the second ring.

"Bud," she pleaded. "Won't you leave this alone now?"

Of course I knew she was talking about the Bayards. "It's a little late. I'm in the middle of an investigation."

"The Bayards think you're out to get them. People are talking about it."

"Talk is what we do in this town."

"Bud, it isn't a joke. You can't fight them."

"I'm not fighting them. I'm just doing my job."

"For your mother's sake!"

Peggy had caught me by surprise. "Phyllis?" I said stupidly.

"They will destroy you. And they will destroy Carl, too."

Leave it to Peggy to see the practical side. I hadn't considered it in those terms. But yes, the Bayards would not be above using Carl to get at me. And Carl would oblige. Certainly. He was their man.

"You don't want that," Peggy said.

No, I didn't want to see Carl destroyed. Not now, at the end of his career, before he got that bridge named for him.

"Oh, Bud. Think about it."

I didn't tell her that's all I had been thinking about. I said I would stop by for coffee soon, and once again she admonished me: "Be careful."

I went out and got in the Buick and drove up the Keys. Away from the turmoil, the taint of politics in a small town at the end of the road. If I had my life to live over again, I thought, casting my eyes over the track of water dotted with shimmering uninhabited islands that grew recklessly, I would have left here. Gone on to another life free of the past. Escaped. The way Phyllis escaped when she arrived here. Or Captain Billy when he left us.

That was a haunting memory. Whenever I saw young men whose fathers I knew, it never failed to surprise me how much alike they were in their manners and speech. So much of life was imitative, and I suppose I had lived always with some subconscious fear of imitating Captain Billy.

I made it a hundred miles, as far as the upper Keys, where I spent two nights in a motel, going out for meals and to sit at the edge of the water and listen to the wind coming across Florida Bay, whistling like a siren song tempting me away. The temptation came too late. I was like those mangrove islands, shimmering in the background, rooted fast into these shallow waters, twisted and twining back on themselves, until there was no place to turn but home.

40

Apart from two lone sailors in khaki uniforms who were sitting at the bar, the Club was empty Friday night. I chatted with Ronnie over a club soda until Harry came in. He was in a lather over some tourist chick he'd scored with who was on her way out of town in the morning. It looked like it was going to be one of those slow nights, the beginning of the summer doldrums, so I gave Harry the night off.

I sat down at the piano and led off with "I Get Along Without You Very Well." The sailors never looked up from their beer. I was in the middle of "Am I Blue" when she came in. She sat at the end of the bar and gave me her wave, the fingers of her left hand closing over her palm.

I played for another twenty minutes before the sailors left, then took a break.

Casey stood up, putting her hands on my shoulders for an awkward embrace. Since I'd been playing here, she'd never been in the Club that I could remember.

"What brings someone like you to a joint like this?" I took my revitalized club soda from Ronnie and steered Casey out to the open-air deck overlooking the city.

"I came by your place a couple of times but you weren't around," Casey said. We stood leaning against the balcony ledge, watching the traffic as it crawled along Duval Street. The blare from a boom box filtered up seven stories, assaulting us. "I thought you'd probably need some time."

"To sober up?" We didn't look at each other.

"Bud, don't. You know I've always given you my support, but I can't do for you what you're unwilling to do for yourself."

She said it in a way that didn't sound preachy, and I didn't object. "I've quit drinking," I said.

"I'm glad." Her tone was matter-of-fact.

"But you don't believe it."

"I believe you haven't had a drink in a few days."

"But not that I'll never have another one."

"I don't know that I'll never have another one," Casey said emphatically. "It's an ongoing process."

"You think I should go to meetings."

"Bud, I didn't come here to talk about your drinking."

Out across the town, beyond Duval Street, the treetops were billowy and dark as storm clouds. Here and there a familiar church spire or tower breaking through, and everywhere landmarks that held distant memories; not a few of them rejects. "Well," I said, "how about Alex Farquar then?"

"Yes. That is one of the things I came to talk about."

This wasn't part of our routine. Since our relationship was undefined, I never meddled in her outside interests. We were friends, and sometime lovers. It was what I wanted and what Casey could deal with given our differences. It seemed easy. Until now. Until Alex Farquar.

"It isn't exactly what you think," Casey said.

"What it is, is none of my business, I guess."

"Well, I saw you on your bike the other night."

"I was out for a ride."

"Alex asked me out a couple of times. We went to dinner. That's the extent of it."

"Did he tell you about New Orleans?"

"No. I refused to talk with him about you. What happened?"

I told her.

"Bud, that's terrible. I'm sorry."

"It's worse." We continued to avoid each other's eyes, still looking out across the city. "Someone in the state attorney's office may have tipped off the defendants that I was going there to pick up a witness."

"Who would do that? And why?"

"Someone who's working both sides of the street. Probably doubling his income."

"Bud, Alex was persistent. Believe me, there's nothing to it. It was dinner."

"I'm not accusing you of anything. Or him. You're both free people."

"But you're suspicious."

"If you're seeing Farquar, you need to know. I get a lot of work out of that office."

"Bud, I won't see him. I don't want to see him."

In the darkness I smiled. "It's all right, Casey. I'm not making demands. Just be careful."

I turned and faced the barroom. Half a dozen people had come in and were sitting at tables facing the piano. Casey leaned her head against me. "Nothing is ever simple, is it?" she asked.

I didn't say anything. Nothing was simple right now. I felt like a man walking around in a weighted dive suit. Every move had to be thought out. I tried to remember if life had ever been simple and recalled maybe three or four summers when I was a kid before I became aware of the turmoil in my parents' lives.

"I've got to go back to work," I said.

We walked inside together. Casey squeezed my arm before I went to the piano, sat down, and hovered over "Every Time We Say Good-bye." When I looked up, Casey was standing at the back of the room waiting for the elevator. The doors opened and she was gone.

41

In the dark, I fumbled with my keys to the Yale lock on the back door. It was about one-thirty in the morning. I'd stopped playing half an hour ago when the few remaining drinkers had left the Club and, after hanging around to keep Ronnie company while she cleaned up, made my way home. I like this town at this time of the night. Coming home from a club date when the town is only semiconscious and the heat of the day has dissipated, I have always felt a certain refuge in these dark hours.

In the years I lived with Peggy, never a night person, I would often open a cold beer after a session and sit out in a lawn chair, gazing at the sky.

Maybe it was the association with my summer nights as a kid. I remember them as being the rare time when we gathered as a family. Captain Billy was for the most part an absentee father. He had relinquished parenting to Phyllis. Gone early in the morning most of the days when he was with City Electric, and out on his boat evenings and weekends, my father was seldom around for meals. So it was those summer nights when Carl and I could stay up late that I remember sitting on the porch with them, listening to Captain Billy talk about his fishing expeditions, or politics.

The memory of those nights is charged with a sense of excitement as electric as the slow, jagged blue flashes of lightning that frequently rent the summer sky, freezing us in our places, often shutting down the power, so that we would sit in total darkness until Phyllis brought out a candle.

Just as I got the key into the lock and the door open, one of those nights came back to me in startling clarity. Captain Billy was sitting on a canvas chair on the porch, a candle glowing in a glass hurricane lantern on a table next to him. Phyllis sat in the swing, Carl and I on either side of her. Captain Billy may have had a couple more drinks than usual because he was wound up and going on about his favorite subject, the Bayards.

Again I hear my father's voice. Self-satisfied and chuckling as he relates one of the many anecdotes that have accumulated around the Bayard family over the years. He is telling a story about the patriarch, John T., who had a reputation as a notorious womanizer. His wife, Ann, had caught her husband with someone young enough to be his daughter.

"Oh, Bill, not in front of the boys!" Phyllis said.

My father scoffed in a way that was peculiarly his. "Oh, why not. I hear Peter takes after his old man. Isn't that right, Carl?"

I wasn't yet in junior high but Carl, and Peter, both five years older, were probably in their last year of high school.

"There's a girl he likes." Carl's voice had changed, but he was still testing it, measuring it against Captain Billy's.

"Who's that?" Phyllis asked.

"Just some girl," Carl replied. "You wouldn't know her." In other words an outsider. The way Phyllis herself had been.

"What does her father do?" Phyllis probed, her curiosity engaged, but it was also a way, I'm sure, of deflecting Captain Billy.

Captain Billy was splitting himself with laughter.

"Bill, what is so funny?" my mother asked.

"Like father, like son," Captain Billy managed to mutter between laughs. "The old man is bird-dogging his son's girlfriends."

"Please, Bill."

"Carl, did you hear about this?"

"No," Carl said.

"This is just a sick rumor," Phyllis said.

"Sick or not, Ann caught them together in John T.'s car."

"That doesn't prove anything."

"If you know John T., it does."

There was another flash of lightning and several seconds later the silencing boom of thunder. Moments later, when the rain began, Carl got up and went inside.

"Bill, I wish you wouldn't do that," Phyllis said. "He's very sensitive."

"Just the facts of life," Captain Billy said.

The facts of life. If he could only have known that half a century later the facts from that harmless conversation would provide the motivation I was looking for to go after the Bayards.

What a trick our memories play on us, that this should enter my consciousness right now. I have heard, or read someplace, that every sound we make gets recorded in space. For all time.

Our voices, our words outlived us.

Lila. If there were only some way to tap into her voice; I wanted to hear her, but it seemed to have been silenced when her sister, Virginia, died. I went in and sat down at the piano where Lila's picture rested on the music rack. Killing me softly . . . with your smile. There were so many more questions now.

42

The annual benefit dance Portia Villani had asked me to play was less than a week away, on Thursday. Saturday morning I called around to make sure that arrangements had been made for the piano and amplifying equipment I would need. Then I called Judge Watson.

On weekends I knew that Just, an enthusiastic fisherman, liked to spend time on the water. This morning, however, a squall line was hanging off the southeastern horizon and we'd been getting intermittent rain accompanied by strong gusts of wind all morning. The weather forecast included a small-craft advisory, so I called to see if the judge would like to go to lunch.

"Can't make it today," Just said. "Weather permitting, I'm taking the boat out tomorrow, though, if you want to go fishing."

It had been years since I'd been on a fishing boat. Captain Billy used to take me out once in a while on the *Low Blow,* and I would help the mate bait and set the outriggers while clients sat in the deck chairs, drinking beer and waiting for something to strike their own baited hooks. We trolled along the edge of the Gulf Stream, the boat wallowing in the dark blue waters, as our eyes scanned astern for a sailfish or a marlin to break the surface and jump our lines. I found it monotonous, and on the times when those big fish did take the bait and the mate set the hook and handed the rod to a beery-eyed client, who fought the fish for a couple of hours, sad. My stomach was always queasy, and the sight of one of those monstrous fish lying dead on the deck of the boat, bleeding, the color draining from its body, left me filled with a kind of nameless dread.

I never said anything to Captain Billy, who would only have laughed. He never seemed quite so happy as on days when he caught fish and had his picture taken with his client, standing on the dock next to a fish that hung from a block and tackle, its weight chalked on its ghastly side.

The morning I was called at the police station to come to the boat where I found my father lying on his stomach in the wheelhouse, his head in a puddle of blood, I felt that same sense of dread. It was as if there were some tragic fate awaiting those of us who had participated in the mindless slaughter of these creatures, beginning with my father; some retribution that would be claimed for our arrogance.

From the day I carried Captain Billy's body from the *Low Blow,* I never again set foot on another deep-sea sport-fishing boat. A few times I had been on powerboats zooming around the harbor, less often on sailboats, but the sea held too much mystery for me, and despite my heritage, I acknowledged my anxiety.

Judge Watson was primarily a fly fisherman who seemed to fish more for the solace of being alone on the water than for anything he might catch, which, in any case, he released once he'd brought it to the boat.

We left at dawn Sunday morning, flying west to the Marquesas over the shallow water of the flats in the judge's ancient twenty-foot skiff with a 150-HP Evinrude hanging off the stern. It had been years since I'd last been here, but it was a primeval scene, unchanged over time except for the debris that reflected our age: styrofoam cups, plastic wrappers, and aluminum cans washed up into the mangroves and deserted dune beaches.

Just maneuvered the skiff back into one of the many lagoons inside the Marquesas, surrounded by mangroves, and cut the engine. The water back here was placid as a lake, an ice sky flushed by the rising sun. Diamondlike projectiles of light shot off the water in the distance where wading birds stood motionless as death, their long-necked, grayish bodies frozen against the backdrop of mangroves. Except for the whisper of wavelets lapping around the chine of the boat, there was absolute silence.

For a moment neither of us moved, taking in the scene, the sudden cessation of sound and activity, before Just set fire to a cigar, then lifted a couple of spinning rods from their rack, handing one to me. It was fitted with a green plastic tube lure, around stainless-steel leader wire that tied onto the line. The tip of a hook glinted through one end of the lure. I recognized a 'cuda rig as I watched Just move up into the bow and begin blind-casting for the powerful, missile-shaped barracuda.

After yesterday's blow the water here, though calm, was still murky, limiting our ability to see the fish, which was why Just was using a spinning rod rather than a fly rod. I stood at the stern and made a few blind casts myself into the mirrored water, but after a few minutes I was content to sit down and watch Just, his back to me, as he cast and retrieved line, a cloud of cigar smoke occasionally billowing over his head.

This kind of fishing had been too still, too tame for Captain Billy. He needed to hear the thump of the engines, be at the wheel to feel the momentum, shouting instructions over the drone of the engines, exercising some measure of control over his sea world. This silent drifting was too haphazard for a man like my father, a man used to imposing himself on nature. The difference between Captain Billy and Just Watson was the difference between night and day, I thought.

Nearly half an hour passed while Just continued casting, without a word and without catching a fish. When he finally came back to the cockpit, the judge grinned. "Bud, I thought you were a fisherman."

"It's been a few years. I was just thinking about Captain Billy, the days on the *Low Blow.*"

"Not quite the same thing."

"A far cry."

"Let's take a look over here. I've caught permit a few times in the past on the south side." Just started the motor and we eased over just above an idle to the other end of the lagoon. Other than a cormorant or two taking off from the water, their black tail feathers dripping water, the wading birds weren't disturbed.

Skittish permit inhabited these shallow waters and fed by nosing into the bottom muck in search of crabs. As they did, their tails sometimes broke the surface, marking their location for a sharp-eyed fisherman.

When we were drifting once more, the motor off, Just picked a live crab from the bottom of a bait bucket and put it on a hook on another spinning rod, then went forward and, dangling the crab over the side, scanned the water. I saw nothing. The tails were dark, like triangular flags, and exceptionally difficult to see against the water.

Moments later, I was amazed when Just flipped back his rod and cast. "See him?" he asked quietly.

"No." I saw the crab land about twenty yards to the front and left of the boat, and as Just began reeling in, there was a sudden splash of water when Just struck the fish. Line began to zing off his reel. Permit were savage fighters, and for the next twenty minutes the two played one another until Just finally brought him alongside the boat, picked him up, and took the hook from his mouth. Then, cradling the fish in both hands, Just gently moved the permit back and forth along the surface of the water, pumping air into its gills. When he was released, the permit darted away.

Sweating, Just came back, got a thermos of coffee, and sat down behind the wheel. "All there is to it," he said.

"Sure. Care to repeat it?"

"Shit. A man gets one or two of those a year, he's lucky. Like looking for a needle in a haystack."

I shook my head as another example came to mind: finding a killer whose victim has been dead for four decades.

43

At ten o'clock we ran over to the lee side of the mangroves and tied off to one of the overhanging branches. Both Just and I had caught and released a couple of barracuda, making it a successful trip in the judge's view. Sitting in the shade and eating sandwiches, we reminisced about the old days when fish were so plentiful you caught all you wanted simply by dangling a line off any of the docks along the harbor.

Was it a more relaxed time then? Was it any easier? Or was that simply nostalgia? Everyone knew each other and there was a certain order that existed then that doesn't seem to exist now. When you wanted something done, you knew whom to go to to get it done. Today the town has become so layered with political brinkmanship it is impossible to know anymore who stands for what. John T. Bayard controlled Key West, indeed, the entire county, as though it were his personal fiefdom. One could disagree with his decisions, as I did, but there was never any question about where he stood.

"What do you remember about John T.?" I asked Just.

"Bayard?" He grinned around a mouthful of ham-and-cheese sandwich.

I nodded. I seemed to recall that Just got his first appointment as a justice of the peace, the early forerunner of our civil court judges. John T. would have been instrumental in making that appointment. While I didn't think Just Watson acknowledged fealty to anyone, I never knew what his personal feelings were regarding the Bayards.

"A powerful man," Just said, swallowing his sandwich. "I hate to see you fighting them, Bud."

"Did you like him?"

"Oh, hell, you couldn't help but like him. You might not agree with him, but his personality was as infectious as a disease. You know that, you knew him."

"Women?"

"Sure, there were plenty of stories about John and women." Just's eyes twinkled as he reached for his thermos. "And not a few about you, too, as I recall."

I ignored that. I was trying to keep to the point, but I could see Just's drift: you couldn't condemn a man's politics simply because he was a womanizer.

"You ever hear of him involved with younger women, schoolgirls?"

Just's expression took on its familiar judicial countenance. "Bud, why don't you tell me what you're getting at."

I hesitated, looking out across the lagoon; the water

that only a few hours ago had been so placid was being stirred by a freshening breeze out of the southeast. You could actually feel the calm being replaced by tension. Then, I told him about my memory of Captain Billy's conversation that night, the possible, and I emphasized *possible,* link, built on John T.'s reputation.

"I think the Bayards were involved somehow in Lila's disappearance, the girl who was killed up by the bat tower in '55."

Just eyed me warily. "You think they killed her?"

I couldn't go that far, but in my mind I had found a slender thread, tenuous, yes, but enough to begin trying to connect some of the pieces. There was, for example, the stranger who was seen at the bar the night of the dance, talking to Lila. Yes, of course it might have been a random killing, some psycho, or a guy she'd met at another time and spurned. The list of possibilities was endless. Among them were the Bayards. Not least of those possibilities was the idea that this was a hired killing. I didn't see any point in mentioning that to the judge.

"Anything is possible," was all I said.

"Have you got any proof? Or is this just suspicion based on the feud you've got going with the Bayards over that motel?"

Sooner or later someone was going to ask that. I'd asked it myself. But I'm not vindictive. Not to the extent of crying murder because the view in my backyard has been messed up, anyway. "No proof," I said. "I'm just trying to follow where the circumstances lead."

Just relit the stub of his cigar. "I'm glad you waited until we got out here to have this conversation," he said through a cloud of smoke. "I wouldn't want to risk being overheard in town. I guess I don't have to tell you what the legal system thinks about circumstantial evidence."

"No, you don't."

"And neither do I have to tell you of the trouble the Bayards can cause you if they get wind of this."

I shook my head.

"And that's going to hamper your investigation. How are you going to get answers to questions you can't ask?"

That was a problem.

"Bud, I can't advise you on this. You may have valid reasons for pursuing the Bayards. But you're going to have a damn hard time sticking them with anything, short of absolute proof. And my guess is that died with Lila Murphy."

Which was why I wanted so badly to hear her voice, even if it were filtered through someone else's.

At nine o'clock on Monday morning I called George Lewis at the city police department.

"Still no luck tracking down Virginia Murphy's people?" I asked.

"None."

"How hard are you trying?"

"Hard enough. There are other things to do around here, you know."

"You get anything at all from Savannah?"

"A rooming house where she was living."

"Got the address handy?"

"Bud, it's a damn good thing you and I go back a ways because you're a needy SOB."

I said I'd wait. George sighed. But he put the phone

down, and when he returned moments later, I wrote down the address and phone number he gave me. As soon as I hung up, the phone rang.

"Gideon, glad I caught you. How are you?" It was Alex Farquar. Chipper and oily as ever. I couldn't believe Casey could be taken in by this guy.

"Okay," I said. I hadn't seen Farquar since I'd blown up about the New Orleans trip. Unless you counted the night I glimpsed him bringing Casey home.

"You busy with anything, Gideon?" He was tentative, testing the waters.

"Depends," I grunted.

"What on?"

"You plugged the leaks in your office?"

"Oh, Gideon, that. No, I believe you're mistaken. In any case, I've got an inquiry out, but it's only been a week."

"Well, then, I'm busy."

"Not available."

"Exactly. Not available."

"Well, Gideon, if you change your mind—"

I hung up before saying something I might regret. Or Casey might regret. This was crazy. Work wasn't exactly lining up at the door. The SA's office still owed me money. I had the check for two grand from Virginia Murphy gathering dust in my desk drawer—which might not be any good now that she was dead—but I could hardly afford to turn down jobs. I had some pride, too damn much pride probably, but I wouldn't work for Alex Farquar. Not with the double bind he'd put me in.

As I walked out to the kitchen, I saw Jack Bayard framed in the glass of the door, coming up onto the porch. Behind him the fence he'd had put up was now covered with graffiti. He was wearing a button-down, short-sleeved shirt and jeans. Jack had a slow, menacing kind of walk that could lull you into thinking he had nowhere to go and all the time in the world to get there.

I opened the door and stood leaning against the jamb. Jack gave me a thin-lipped smile.

"Bud, I'm glad I caught you."

I didn't move, didn't say anything.

"Look, I understand. You were drunk, it cost you a night in jail. It cost me some money, but I don't want to start a war over it."

"Who's starting a war?"

"It's just another motel."

"You're right," I said. "Another one."

"Can we bury the hatchet?"

Jack still had a thick head of hair, curly and graying slightly at the temples. He looked good, robust. Like Peter, Jack had been married to only one woman for many years, but unlike his father no rumors circulated about other women. Still, it was easy to picture him getting what he wanted from any woman, one way or another. However, standing here on my back porch, Jack didn't look like a killer, and I had a hard time imagining him, or Peter, killing anyone. Clint, maybe, but he was barely out of diapers when Lila Murphy was murdered. But I kept telling myself that guys like the Bayards didn't have to get their hands dirty because there was always someone around willing and able to do that work for them. Politics, as we all knew, picked up some strange bedfellows.

"I talked to your brother," Jack said when I didn't reply. "He'd like to see this feud end, too."

"I'm sure he would."

I could picture Carl having to field the same kind of calls I had, trying to explain to friends, people who had known us, my behavior. Once again Tallahassee would become his refuge, a place he could retreat to from the embarrassment of family.

"Well, what about it?" Jack put out his hand.

I shook my head. "There's too many unanswered questions about Lila Murphy."

Jack's hand dropped to his side as if he'd suddenly been burnt. A patina of sweat appeared on his upper lip. "Drop this shit, Bud. You're just making trouble for yourself."

"Did Lila go out with your father?"

"Bud, I'm not answering your questions about that crap. And anytime I see you on Bayard property, I'll have you arrested. I don't like to do this, Bud, because of Carl, but you're not leaving me any choice." Jack turned and stepped off the porch.

"The reason you couldn't get to her was because she was after the successful Bayards and you were still just a kid—like Lila. How'd that make you feel, Jack?"

Jack stopped and did a slow turn, an expression of hatred in his eyes unlike any I'd ever seen in a Bayard. I had unnerved him. At that moment, I thought, if there was something he could have done to me, some physical harm that would go unwitnessed, he would have done it. Yes, he had that capability. As Jack raised his fist, I stepped back into the kitchen and closed the door.

I went to the phone and called a travel agent and booked a flight to Savannah the following morning.

45

Hanging moss and magnolia trees, Savannah was the South. Key West, subtracted from the mainland as it was, more a punctuation mark than verbal text, seemed somehow segregated from this region's identity. Nothing identified the South more than its accent, and the native Keys accent was barely even a distant relative of that in this area of corn pone and cotillions. Captain Billy's people held more in common with the islands, the Caribbean, that mix of English and black that had been part of the westward migration, a migration forced on some and chosen by others.

Phyllis, of course, was pure Southern, not a debutante by any means, but privileged nonetheless. I felt her identity more acutely here, in Savannah, than I had in New Orleans where the atmosphere over the years had been garbled, as it was in Key West. Too many carpetbaggers. I sensed that Savannah was pure, real, however crumbling and seedy. The faintly sour smell of damp pulp still hung in the air from the nearby paper mills, and there was something about the people here that suggested some collective secret, as though they had born witness to something too horrible to share with the rest of the world.

Phyllis had been like that, too. An only child, she had come from South Carolina with a small inheritance soon after her parents died. Her father had had an executive position in the tobacco industry and died of a heart attack in his early fifties. A year later she lost her mother.

Phyllis shared few details of her early life with us, and I always sensed that she had deliberately separated herself from that life, wanting for reasons she could not share to put it behind her. In coming to Key West, she had come to the right place. We Conchs were not much interested in people's backgrounds outside of our own. Phyllis had a lot of years to forget whatever it was she wanted forgotten before I started asking questions sometime in my teens. If Carl, who spent so much more time with her, got more out of Phyllis than I did, he never told me. And Captain Billy, I'm sure, had no interest at all in the state of South Carolina and what went on there before Phyllis entered his life in Key West.

Virginia Murphy also had a secretive streak. I found the boardinghouse where she had lived on Jones Street for the past seven years. It was in a gray brick structure, the brick even with the sidewalk like many in old Savannah. It was a Victorian building that had been divvied up into small apartments and rooms. Virginia's name was still on the intercom.

The woman who managed the boardinghouse lived in her own apartment on the third floor. She came down the stairs and opened the door, clutching a dish towel. She was very thin, and it was hard to tell her age, but I guessed she must have been in her fifties.

"Is it about a room?" she asked.

"No, I'm from Key West. I was a friend of Virginia Murphy's."

She shook her head back and forth, rubbing her hands on the towel. "So sad. The police called here looking for relatives, but Virginia seemed to be all alone in the world."

"What about her stuff?"

"In her room?"

I nodded.

"We got rid of it a couple days ago. She didn't have a lot. It was a furnished room."

"What did you do with it?"

"Most of it went to Sally R."

"Who?"

"The Salvation Army."

I nodded again. "How well did you know Virginia?"

"I've only been here a couple of years. Virginia kept to herself. We talked once in a while. She seemed very lonely."

"Did anyone visit her?"

The woman shook her head. "She had a woman friend who came by every so often, but she lived alone. Really, she stuck pretty much to herself."

"Do you know the friend's name?"

"I'm sorry. I wish I could help."

I stood there while the woman put a finger to her mouth. "Oh, you know," she said after a moment, "I think Virginia went to meetings."

"Meetings?"

"Yes, for people with drinking problems."

Yes, I told her I knew about people like that. Would she by any chance know where she might have attended those meetings. Well, the woman said, the nearest place was over on Abercorn. I thanked her and got in my rental car and drove to a gas station where I stopped and looked up the AA clubs in Savannah. The attendant gave me directions on how to get to the one I found listed on Abercorn, and I set out to my first AA meeting. I thought of Casey and pictured her smiling when I told her I'd been to an AA meeting on behalf of a dead woman.

46

Appropriately, the meeting hall had once been a saloon, which had gone out of business. Many of the furnishings were still in place. The building's owner, himself a friend of AA founder Bill W.'s, someone told me later, had turned it over to AA and a few other self-help groups for a modest monthly rent.

I don't know what I'd expected. A certain amount of self-righteousness, perhaps. But there was none of that. Except for the fact that there was no alcohol, the fifteen or twenty people in here looked like any other group of bar patrons. Men, women—young and old—most of them smoking. The place was deep in a cloud of cigarette smoke, ashtrays overflowing on the tables where they sat on metal fold-up chairs in some loosely structured way facing the bar. Many of them sipped from cans of soft drinks as they listened to the speaker, a bearded man in farmer's overalls who sat in the middle of the long bar. Behind him was an old Budweiser sign, left over from the bar days.

Judging from appearances, they were people from a variety of social positions, from the homeless to the professional. They wore shorts and tattered jeans, dresses and suits. Apart from the smoke the unair-conditioned hall smelled of sweat.

I sat down and listened as the speaker read from a pamphlet each of the twelve steps that ruled this group's life. As I stood in the back listening to the words and trying to imagine making them mine, I let my eyes wander over the people here. Which one of them, if any, might have had the closest relationship with Virginia Murphy? I eliminated the men because I suspected she would confide only in another woman. Among the five women here, there were two whom I judged most likely to have known Virginia.

The meeting, already in progress when I came in, lasted another half hour. Half a dozen people spoke; some of them told stories, shared painful events in their lives that had been caused by alcohol. I recognized the stories because some of them were mine.

When it was over, everyone stood and began to form a circle, joining hands. I was standing at the back and the two people nearest me reached out, inviting me in. Reluctantly, I joined hands with them.

Here I was a stranger, an outsider. These were not my people. And yet they were. Hadn't I recognized myself in their tales of dereliction? They were accepting me, taking me in as one of their own. I was reluctant because I was unable to accept that I had a problem I couldn't solve on my own. I listened to their chorus of voices. "God, grant me the serenity to accept the things I cannot change, the courage to change the things I can, and the wisdom to know the difference."

My hands were clasped firmly for an instant, and then we broke apart. I felt a wave of embarrassment before I spoke. I had changed my mind. There wasn't time to rely on my instincts. I needed to find out if any of these people knew Virginia.

"Excuse me," I called before anyone could leave.

People stopped, turning toward me with puzzled expressions. This was out of the norm. "My name's Gideon." I followed their pattern of using only first names.

"I'm from Key West. And I'm looking for anyone who might have known a friend of mine, Virginia, who I understand sometimes attended these meetings."

There was some hesitation, some whispered conversations before a woman stepped forward. I was relieved that my instincts had been correct. She said, "I'm Sandra," and offered her hand. She had dark hair, and despite a lined face I didn't think she could be much over forty.

"You heard about Virginia?" I asked.

"It was in the paper," Sandra said.

"I'm a private investigator. Virginia hired me to look into a matter that concerned her family when she lived in Key West as a child."

"I knew her, although we weren't close friends." Sandra opened her purse and took out a slip of paper and a pen. "But I do know someone who was close to Virginia." She hurriedly scribbled the number down and handed it to me. "Her name's Carrie Stevens."

"I appreciate it."

"I've gotta go," Sandra said. "Late for work as it is."

I walked with her out onto the street and watched as Sandra got into a Toyota parked at the curb.

I saw a park a couple blocks away and decided to walk down there. It was shady, with park benches beneath large trees. I sat down on one of them and watched a woman play with two young children. The sun, filtered through the massive live oak trees, flecked the manicured lawn with a dappled-gray light. It was peaceful, domestic; all of the things Virginia Murphy hadn't been.

I remembered when Virginia had come to my office after her trip to the detox hospital in Miami in an attempt to get sober, unsure if she wanted to go on with this quest. Virginia had intimated that she felt insignificant beside her beautiful, popular sister. When I asked her about Lila's relationships with boys, though, Virginia couldn't remember any names, any major relationships.

But when I'd suggested to Jack Bayard that maybe he'd been enamored of Lila, spurned by her as she attached herself to the rising young architect in the Bayard family, I had hit a nerve. Jack had become openly hostile. Had I stumbled on the truth? Jack and Lila were the same age, a year older than Virginia. "Lila could have had any boy she wanted," Virginia had said. "They were all after her."

And what about Virginia? The boys were not after her, but was she after them? Had Lila been a rival, maybe even for a Bayard—someone, for example, like Jack?

I sat there in the shade, pushing these thoughts around, watching the kids play until sometime after two when I wandered back to my car and drove downtown to the hotel where I was staying. I went into the coffee shop and had a sandwich, then went up to my room and fell asleep on the bed. I dreamed of my mother. When I awoke, it was late afternoon and I went out for a walk, returning to the hotel at five. At five-thirty I called the number Sandra had given me. No answer. At six I called again and a woman's voice answered.

"Carrie?" I asked.

"Yes."

"My name's Gideon Lowry. I'm from Key West."

"Yes, I wondered when you would call."

47

She suggested we meet in a bar, one nearby my hotel that I had passed on my walk, say in a quarter of an hour. I agreed and gave her a description of myself.

I showered, put on a fresh pair of khakis and a white shirt, and went to meet Carrie. I was sitting at the bar, a club soda with lime in my hand, when she came in and walked straight to me. She was full-figured, with short dark hair combed in a wave to the side, a couple of tendrils falling over one eye. She wore a Western-style shirt tucked into slacks. She had an elfish oval face and appeared to be a good bit younger than Virginia.

"Gideon?" She gave me her hand and sat down on the barstool next to me. "I would have known you even without the description."

The bartender came by and said hello to Carrie. "Martini?" he asked.

"Don't forget the two olives," Carrie said.

"Another club soda?"

I nodded, handing him my glass.

"You don't drink?" Carrie asked.

"Not anymore," I replied.

"I see. Because I thought Virginia mentioned that you'd had drinks together."

"Which, I take it, is how you knew me."

"Virginia called me from the clinic she checked herself into in Miami."

"She never mentioned you."

"I know. Sandy called and said you'd been to a meeting and she had given you my number."

The bartender put a martini glass in front of Carrie, two bulbous green olives lying in the clear gin, and the club soda in front of me.

"Cheers!" Carrie said.

We touched glasses.

"You know there are in the world people who can take a drink without falling apart. I'm one of them. I think it put a strain on my relationship with Virginia."

"Why?"

Carrie smiled and showed yellowing teeth. "If you drank with her, you should know. When she was drinking, it was all downhill from the first drink. When she wasn't, she didn't want to be around anyone who was." She took another sip of her martini. "I'm glad to see you're not that way."

"I'm a drunk. It finally caught up with me."

Carrie shrugged and smiled again. "Well, fire away. What do you want to know?"

"Virginia didn't have any family?"

"None. At least none that would claim her. There might be some cousins around, but she hadn't had any contact with them in years."

"So you were the closest person to her?"

"Close?" She mused over the word. "At one time we were lovers. But you probably guessed that."

It had been in the back of my mind.

"It's all right. You're too sensitive to ask. We hadn't been to bed together in five years."

"But you still spent time together?"

"Off and on. We still cared for each other even though we were no longer in love." Carrie laughed. "So what is it you want to know?"

"What made her tick?"

Carrie shook her head. "Oh, God, she was complicated. She went to a shrink for a while who thought she was frozen."

"Frozen?"

"She used to tell me about it. He claimed she was suffering from chronic grief."

Frozen. It was an apt description of Virginia, I thought, thinking back on the times I'd been with her. She was so constricted, done up in that "habit," not so much like a nun as Ronnie had suggested, but rather a mummy. Virginia had been wrapped so tightly, physically and emotionally, I thought, she could barely move. Frozen.

"Personally," Carrie went on, "I thought he was a pompous ass. All that business about guilt."

"What guilt?"

"That Virginia felt inferior to Lila, and the wrong person died."

"Virginia certainly felt inferior."

"Yes, I suppose there was something to it, but in my opinion it was a lot simpler than that. Virginia was a drunk. She had obsessions. Like I said, what makes some people drunks and others not, I don't know. What about you? Do you have some deeply troubled past that sent you to the bottle?"

Good question. Had my unresolved relationships with Captain Billy and Phyllis driven me to drink? I had never thought so before, but after the past few weeks I was beginning to wonder. "I don't know," I replied.

"Well, I can tell you that Virginia when she was sober was pretty even-keeled. Eccentric maybe, but stable. Years of drinking just kept pushing her back."

"How did she live?"

"You mean financially?"

I nodded.

"She had a small trust fund and the insurance she got after her parents died."

"So what was her obsession after all these years? What do you think?"

Carrie downed the last of her martini and, smiling, said, "I think she thought she knew who killed Lila."

48

The bar was clubby with a lot of wood paneling and framed prints of ducks. The wall behind the mahogany bar was brick and had a large antique mirror in the center bounded by bottles on shelves to either side, and below it. Several antique Hunter fans with round light globes made of clouded glass hung from long extension rods attached to the stamped-tin ceiling.

Carrie ate the olives from her glass, then ordered another martini. "Don't worry, this is it. Two's my max."

"I'm not counting."

Carrie laughed. "Virginia liked you. I can see why." I got up and went to pee. When I came back, there was a fresh club soda on the bar.

"What do you want me to do with her remains?" I asked.

Carrie looked puzzled for a second, then said, "Oh, God! The ashes?"

I nodded. "I can have her sent to you."

Carrie seemed to think about it for a moment. "No. She should stay in Key West. That's where she spent most of her time even if it was only in her head."

"How close were you?"

"Do you think I'm cold, Gideon? Well, I loved her. But everything changes, doesn't it? We were like sisters. Now that's ironic, isn't it? I'm not going to spend the rest of my life grieving, though. Not the way Virginia did."

"She must have been difficult."

"You know what it's like living with an alcoholic. Going through the sweats. The paranoia. The depression. Waking up in the middle of the night with someone who has the screaming meemies."

"Some of that's familiar."

"Sometimes you hear stuff that doesn't make sense. A lot of it you learn to tune out."

I suppose I was hoping for a revelation that would give a name to Lila's killer, the kind of admission that would come from the depths of the subconscious of her traumatized youth. After all, I had remembered something from my past the other day, some long-stored episode, one of many on the porch at William Street. Meaningless at the time it happened, its significance only unearthed by augers chipping away at corroded memories.

"You began putting some of the pieces together?" I said.

"Not exactly. It was more a feeling I had. Back when we were first getting to know each other, and that was fifteen years ago."

I felt a keen disappointment. Perhaps I had hoped for too much.

"Was she drinking so heavily then?"

"No. The drinking was progressive." Carrie touched my arm. "Don't look so glum."

"So what made you feel so strongly that Virginia knew something?"

"The last time I talked to her she thought she'd come up with something."

"When was that?"

"It must have been the night she died."

I was playing that night and Virginia had come up to the Club. I remember she left early. It was the night she gave me the check, but I didn't recall her being particularly excited by anything. "Do you remember what time she called?"

"Probably around ten or eleven. That's usually when we talked."

So whatever Virginia found out came after she left the Club.

"Did she tell you what it was?"

"She was going to meet someone."

"That night?"

"She didn't say."

"A name?"

"Bared."

"What?"

"Bared," Carrie repeated in her soft Southern accent.

And I heard Virginia. Bared. Bayard. It was the way it was pronounced here.

"Bayard," I said.

Carrie shook her head and smiled. "Mean anything?"

I smiled back. "It certainly does."

"Well, good. Because it was something I'd heard her say before when she was in one of her rants."

"Something you heard and tuned out?"

"Yes. Except I confronted her about it, along with other stuff she would say, but she had no idea what I was talking about. She was a blackout drinker."

Another link in the chain. Now all I had to do was connect Jack with Virginia that night.

Carrie finished her martini. "I'm hungry," she said. "And I have some questions."

"Your turn to fire away."

"Why are you bothering with this now that she's dead?"

I took her to dinner and told her. We ate in a crowded place near the embankment overlooking the river. I talked about Phyllis and Captain Billy and my brother, Carl, and the way that the overlapping of Virginia's life and mine had opened up too many questions about my own past for me to ignore simply because Virginia was dead. I wanted to know what had happened to her, to Lila, but I was also hoping to learn something about myself.

In less than two weeks I had been away from my hometown more than at any time since Korea. From the air, as the small twin-engine plane glided in over the Gulf before banking to the east on final approach, I looked down at the city and felt a heaviness, an awareness of gravity, as though my heart were a weight pushing me down. Below, there was a sparkle of sand, like gold dust, over the shallow banks across from the harbor, and tall masts like accusing fingers pointed heavenward from the decks of sailboats at anchor.

From the airport I drove the Buick across town and parked in the city parking lot. I walked up to George Lewis's office and claimed the remains of Virginia Murphy. She was in a wooden box about the size of a cigar box, and her personal effects were in a printed-cloth satchel, a true carpetbag, which had belonged to her.

George didn't question my authorization, seeming to sense that I knew what I was doing and was in no mood to banter.

I drove home, parked on the side street, and carried my funereal cargo up Duval Street and in the front door. I had given up using the back door, thereby avoiding as much as possible the vision that my people deemed progress.

Tom came out of the desk drawer to greet me, yawning, arching his striped back, his tail quivering as if his neutered body could still spray. I placed the box on the piano above Lila's picture and set the carpetbag on the floor in my closet. Then I went back to my office, opened the blinds, and sat down at my desk. Ignoring the insistent red blink of the answering machine, I put my feet up, leaned back in the swivel chair with my arms bracing my head, and stared at the used-car lot across the street, the prices painted white on the cars' windshields. Red, white, and blue pennant flags flapped on a line around the perimeter of the lot.

I wanted a drink. I wanted a drink as badly as I had wanted anything in my life. Yesterday at this time I'd been in an AA meeting and a few hours later had sat in a bar with a woman who drank martinis. I truly believed then that I would never drink again. I put my feet on the floor and leaned forward to open the drawer where I kept a bottle before remembering that I'd poured everything down the drain last week.

I felt clammy, my shirt stuck to my body where I'd broken out in a sweat.

There was a bar a couple blocks away, or I could go next door to the Cuban *grocería* and grab a sixpack. As I was fumbling for my wallet to check my finances, the phone rang. I thought about not answering it. It rang again. There was a twenty-dollar bill in my wallet. I stood up as the phone rang a third and then a fourth time, but just as the answering machine clicked on, some impulse made me pick up the receiver.

"Bud, I've been trying to get you for a couple of days. I was worried."

Casey. "Been out of town," I said.

"I need to see you."

"What about?"

"Alex. It's important."

"I was just on my way out the door."

"It's my lunch hour. I can come by right now."

I swiped at the sweat on my face. I was soaked. "I need a drink."

Casey hesitated. "Bud, give me five minutes. I'll be there." Her voice was firm, concerned. She knew what she was dealing with.

I hung up and stripped off my shirt. In the bathroom I splashed my face with water, then took a towel and dried my body. My hands shook. I put the towel around my neck and walked out to the kitchen. In the refrigerator I found an opened can of Coke that had gone flat. I was chugging that when she came in.

"How bad is it?"

"Bad enough," I said.

"Sit down."

"What?"

"Sit down."

I sat down on one of the kitchen chairs. Casey lifted the towel from my neck and began to massage my shoulders and back. Under her touch some of the weight I'd felt earlier coming into Key West began to lift.

Casey ran her fingers through my chest hair. "I made a mistake," she said.

"What kind of a mistake?"

"I misjudged Alex. You were right. He is a creep."

"It's all right. We all get taken in once in a while."

"Forgive me?"

"There's nothing to forgive."

"God, is there hope for any of us?" Her fingers began to undo my belt buckle.

The answer of course was no, unless you believed in some form of afterlife, which I didn't. The only hope, I suppose, was getting through this life with some redeeming grace. Casey and I went to the bedroom and made love, silently seeking redemption in each other's eyes.

Portia Villani was in the hospital. She had fallen and broken her hip a day or two after our last visit. In the afternoon I drove out to the hospital on Stock Island to see her. The woman who I'd seen on the stairway in the Villani mansion that last time was seated in a chair beside Portia's bed, holding her hand.

The decline in Portia's appearance in such a short time was disturbing. She had withered. Without the aid of cosmetics her wrinkled face was sallow, and her eyes, having lost their luster, were like tarnished pennies. I wasn't sure she even recognized me. Her hair, which had always been perfectly coiffed when I had seen her, was thin and lay in limp strands on her pillow so that her bare scalp shone through like a baby's.

"Mrs. Villani," I said. "I just heard. I've been out of town."

Her eyes focused for a moment and she managed a trace of a smile. "Gideon, this is my daughter Charity." Her voice was feeble.

I nodded at the woman, who smiled shyly before turning back to her mother.

"Is there anything I can do?" I asked.

Portia moved her head resignedly against the pillow as her eyes fluttered and closed.

I told Charity I would stop back later. I touched Portia's thin forearm. Her skin was cold and dry.

I drove back into town and drove around my block twice hunting for a parking place. Finally, I said to hell with it and drove down to the garage four blocks away, where I left the Buick for its overdue oil change and a tune-up. From there I walked up to Smith Lane to Big Betty's.

A young woman with a stack of freshly laundered, folded sheets was just going up the stairs. She paused, her hand on the railing when I came in.

"Is Jane around?" I asked.

"Oh." She sounded relieved that I knew someone here, that she didn't have to explain that this was a women-only establishment. "I think she's in the kitchen. You can go on back."

I walked past the desk down the narrow, carpeted hallway and came to an old-fashioned kitchen with an oak table in the center of the tiled floor and six sculpted Victorian chairs around it. Heavy copper pots and pans hung from hooks on a rack suspended from the ceiling. Steam was rising from the spout of an industrial-sized teakettle on a gas burner.

"Jane?"

The swinging door to a pantry opened and Jane

stepped into the kitchen with a tray on which was a box of Earl Grey jasmine-scented tea, a teapot, and some cups. She put the tray down on the table, then brushed a strand of hair from her face, studying me. "Gideon, right?"

"Yes. I have another question for you."

"I was just making afternoon tea for the guests. Would you like a cup?" She was wearing a denim skirt and a sleeveless white blouse.

"Please. Two sugars." The driving impulse for a drink that had come over me a few hours ago was gone, thanks once again to Casey, but I found I had a craving for sugar.

"Sit down," Jane said. "Is there any more information on Virginia?"

I pulled out a chair from the table. "I located a close friend of hers in Savannah."

"Oh, I'm glad." I watched Jane pour some hot water from the kettle into the teapot, rinse it, then put a tablespoon of the Earl Grey into the pot before filling it with water and putting it back on the tray.

The young woman who had directed me back here came in and got a lemon from the refrigerator. She sliced some thin rounds and decorated a plate with them, which she added to the tray. Jane brought over a couple of mugs, spooned two teaspoons of sugar in one, then poured some tea into both, and handed the sugared one to me. The other woman left with the tray.

"Now, where were we?" Jane sat down across the table.

"I'm checking to see if Virginia had any phone calls while she was here? Would you have a record of that?"

"I'm pretty sure the police found something in her room. Didn't they tell you?"

I sipped my tea, nodded vaguely, and rebuked myself

for not asking Jane about this the first time I'd talked to her. I suppose I was thinking Virginia knew no one here, or that I would get that information from the police. The truth was, I wasn't thinking.

I remembered going to George Lewis and asking him about the investigation. The day following Virginia's death he'd sent the two beefcakes who'd muscled me over here to question Jane and go through Virginia's room. But when I asked, George had said nothing about phone calls, which he would have known about because I did remember him saying he had walked the beefcakes through the preliminary investigation.

"How does the phone system work?" I asked.

"Each of the rooms has a phone, and up until ten someone is on the desk taking calls and transferring them to rooms."

"And after that?"

"An answering machine takes any messages."

Virginia had been in the Club that night until at least ten, I thought. I was sure that she would have told me if she'd had a call of any significance prior to that.

So when she'd come back here from the Club, there'd been a message. She'd gone to her room, phoned, and met someone—Bared?—who'd come here, and she had taken him to her room. Possible? Anything was possible, but I couldn't imagine Jack Bayard leaving a message for someone he was going to kill. Even if he didn't have murder in mind and only wanted to talk to her, Jack would have been more careful.

If it was Jack Bayard, then that explained why George Lewis would have withheld information from me about a phone call. The Bayards, as usual, got preferential treatment—just as they had during the investigation of Lila's death.

"I don't suppose you'd have any record of Virginia's incoming calls?"

"It depends," Jane said. "We have a book and we log in phone messages in duplicate. Once a book is filled, we throw it out and start a new one. I'll check for you."

Jane walked out to the front desk and returned after a moment carrying a book of phone messages, the kind sold at office supply stores. She put it on the table and thumbed through it. White rectangular message sheets printed with the date, time, caller, message, and number to call attached to yellow duplicate sheets.

"What was the date then?" Jane asked.

"About three weeks ago."

Jane looked through the book for a few minutes. "Here it is." She turned the book around and put her finger on one of the yellow sheets on the page.

There was Virginia's name and room number, a phone number to call, but no name. The call had been made at 8:10 P.M. the night Virginia was killed.

"There's no name here," I said.

"They didn't leave a name."

"Isn't that unusual, a number without a name?"

"They may not have left a number either, but we have caller ID here."

"What?"

"All incoming calls get recorded without the caller knowing it. You'd be surprised at the number of hate calls a place like this gets. It offers us some protection."

I smiled. "So I see," I said.

51

The call had come from the Bayard Cement office up the Keys at the quarry. The link was now cemented—*Buy Bayard by the Yard*, and I was prepared to, even though, without a name, there was nothing to conclude that Jack Bayard, or Clint or Peter for that matter, had made the call. It should have been enough, however, to start an inquiry, a line of questioning, which the police apparently had not done. Should I confront George Lewis? If he was protecting the Bayards, he would certainly tell them what I knew.

In the hackneyed words of Yogi Berra, it was déjà vu all over again. First Frank Paine; now George Lewis.

From Big Betty's I walked over to the courthouse, half a block away. Judge Watson's court had just recessed for the afternoon, and I found Webb Conners hanging around the clerk's office ragging Wilma Patterson.

At one time, it would be fair to say, Webb and I had been best of friends. We had gone through school together and hung together when I returned from Korea. Over the years, marriages—mine, not his (Webb had been married to the same woman for twenty-five years)—had probably done more to alter our relationship than anything else.

While I was married to Peggy, we all used to eat together at least once a week, play pinochle, go to the movies, that kind of thing, and occasionally when both Webb and I had the same day off, the two of us would get together for a beer or two in the afternoon at the Garden of Palms.

I could now see that apart from time and other commitments, our relationship had changed primarily because of me. After Peggy, I became less stable, and to someone as steady as Webb, even volatile. Though they tried, I know that both Webb and his wife, Judy, found the succeeding Mrs. Lowrys (neither of whom had been local women) incompatible.

Judy and Peggy have remained close friends over the years, but while Webb and I would do anything for each other, there is a distance between us now that is beyond either of our abilities to bridge. I trusted him, however, in a way that I would not have trusted George Lewis.

Wilma managed to glimpse me around Webb's considerable girth, which was blocking the doorway. "Mind your back, Webb," Wilma said. "The guy behind you looks dangerous."

Webb turned, stepping out of the doorway. "Bud. How goes it?"

"I was in the area. Thought I'd see if you had a minute."

Webb looked at his watch. "I'm done for the day, I just got out of court. How about I buy you some pie and a cup of coffee?"

"Another piece of pie, Webb, and you won't fit in the door," Wilma said.

Webb shrugged and went down the hallway. Wilma winked at me as I turned to follow him.

We went into Yesterday's and sat in a booth next to the window. True to his word, Webb ordered a piece of coconut cream pie and coffee. I opted for coffee only.

"What's on your mind, Bud?"

"Between you and me, right?"

"Absolutely. You know you can trust me."

I was counting on that. "I just came from Big Betty's."

"The lezzie place on Smith Lane?"

I nodded. "A woman died there a few weeks ago. Virginia Murphy."

Webb had a blank look on his face that gradually turned to pained recognition as the waitress put down the two coffees and the pie. "Bud, I can't believe you're still—"

"Believe it," I said, maybe a little too sharply. Webb looked hurt. "Listen. Someone from Bayard's called Virginia at eight-ten the night she died."

"Bayard's, huh?" Webb shook his head. "I'll listen to you, Bud, but I have to tell you I hate to see you doing this to yourself. You keep going down this road and it's going to be worse for you than a night in jail. A lot worse."

"I don't have any choice."

Webb stared at me, his jaw moving slowly as he chewed his pie. "You still drinking?"

"I quit. I haven't had a drink since that night."

Webb nodded. "All right, Bud. Go ahead and tell me."

"George Lewis found a phone message slip in Virginia's room after she was killed. The caller's number was on it, no name, but the phone number was Bayard Cement."

"And what does that prove?"

"Not a damn thing."

"Well, at least we agree on something."

"But why would someone, *anyone,* be calling Virginia Murphy from Bayard's. A woman who just got into town and hasn't been here in forty years?"

"I can't answer that, Bud. But the fact remains, it doesn't prove anything."

"It's too coincidental. And why didn't Lewis investigate it?"

"Who says he didn't?"

"Well, I talked to him and asked him if he had any leads, any information at all."

Webb snorted. "He's going to tell you, Bud? Everybody in town knows you've had a hard-on for years for the Bayards. I even heard the other day that Jack came over and tried to smooth things out between the two of you, and you blew him off."

"Do me a favor."

"Bud, I'm telling you right now I won't go out on any damn limb for you over this."

"See what you can find out about that call. If Jack, or anybody out there, was questioned about it."

Webb sighed. "I'll try, but I'm not going to get drug into this battle."

"And I'm not going to watch another investigation go the way Lila Murphy's did under Frank Paine."

52

I walked home and called Paul Murchison, the medical examiner for the Keys in the 1950s. It was still a little early for the cocktail hour and his voice sounded scratchy, but clear. He remembered me: "Oh, yes. At the Westerbys. You were asking about the young lady killed up at the bat tower years ago."

"Yes, I'm still looking into that."

"How's it going?"

"Hard to say. I wonder if I could get you to speculate on something."

"What's that?"

"A reason for not performing an autopsy."

Murchison hesitated a moment, then said, "I thought we went over that. As I recall, it was not done at the request of the family."

"A request that was relayed to your office from the sheriff, Frank Paine, I think you said."

"God, I can't be sure of the exact sequence, but I believe it was something like that."

"Well, in general, what other reasons would there be for not doing it?"

Murchison hesitated again. "Hmm, well, if it was obviously death by natural causes, or the cause was apparent and it wasn't a question of murder. You know, so there wasn't going to be a trial with the need for evidence. That kind of thing."

I leaned back in my chair, the phone cradled next to my ear. A couple was actually looking at one of the cars for sale in the lot across the street. The salesman in a short-sleeved, white shirt stood leaning against the side of one car. I picked up a paper clip and bent it into different shapes between my thumb and forefinger until it lost its definition.

"Suppose it was deliberately blocked," I said. "Say you've already got a good idea what the cause of death was but someone doesn't want an autopsy done for what else it might reveal."

"Just speculating," Murchison said.

"Right. That's what we're doing, speculating."

"It's anyone's guess. Maybe the deceased had some illness, a fatal disease. Anything. A young lady like the one in question could have been pregnant. The list of possibilities is endless."

Pregnant.

I suppose it had been ticking away in the back of my mind ever since I'd recalled that night on the porch at

William Street during that long-ago spring thunderstorm. Jack Bayard creaming his jeans over Lila Murphy, and other members of his family perhaps coming too close. So to speak. Lila, the pretty, ambitious opportunist looking for a way to put the squeeze on the Bayard family. Peter, the rising young architect. Or John T., the patriarch of this clan, expanding his territory?

Had Lila's family known any of this?

I was grasping for conclusions that were probably out of my reach. But it made sense. The times then were so different from now. What was commonplace behavior today would have created a scandal sufficient to bring down the Bayards back then.

"If she had been pregnant," I asked Murchison, "how difficult would it have been to prove paternity in those days?"

"Oh, it would depend, of course, upon the degree of decomposition and when she was impregnated."

"The body was found after a week."

"Yes, that's right. Well, it would not have been impossible."

"And proving paternity?"

"Yes, we could have done that back then, too."

After thanking him for his information, I hung up and went into the kitchen and ate a couple of Milky Ways I'd bought on the way home. Then I got on my bike and rode over to Peggy's. I didn't think Jake would be home yet; even though we were friendly enough, and I'm sure Peggy, who was incapable of deception, always told him whenever I stopped by, I preferred to speak to her alone.

Barbara, of course, was there, and I could hear the sound of scales being played on the piano as I rode up.

"Bud," Peggy said, coming to the door as I got off my bike, "I was just thinking about you."

"No good, I imagine."

"I just realized I hadn't seen you in a while. Not since before that incident, and I was wondering how you were doing is all."

The "incident." The way Peggy would forever remember it. She stood behind the screen door, one hand on the aluminum scrollwork. She had on a pair of baggy shorts that did nothing to hide her fleshy thighs, which I noticed were marked with a light crazing of varicose veins.

"Peggy, I wonder if I could talk to you out here for a minute."

"Of course." She looked back, apparently at Barbara, whose playing went uninterrupted, then stepped outside. We stood beneath the avocado tree whose ancient branches spread across the yard with their new green leaves and flowering buds; those surviving the birds and wind would in the fall become avocados. When they ripened, Peggy always saw to it I got all the pears I wanted—alligator pears we Conchs called them.

"What is it, Bud?" She wore a familiar look of worry. "You don't look well. Have you lost weight?"

I had dropped a few pounds and I hadn't shaved. I was still feeling a little shaky. "I'm fine."

"I know it's none of my business, but I hope you're not drinking anymore."

"Nor any less." I smiled and so did Peggy. It was an old joke between us that wasn't very funny. "I haven't had a drink since I was arrested. Peggy, I want to know about Frank Paine."

She began rubbing her fingers. "Oh, Bud, why are you doing this? Frank is dead. Phyllis is dead. Leave them be."

"We're all going to be dead soon enough. But until that time there are things I want to know."

"I've told you all I know about Frank and your mother, Bud."

"I doubt it." Peggy had always been such a caretaker. She never wanted bad things to happen to people, and when things did happen, she would do whatever she could to act as if they hadn't. Ignoring adversity was Peggy's way of protecting herself from conflict.

Peggy put her hands to her face. "They were good people."

"Who?" I thought she was trying to change the subject.

"Frank and Phyllis."

Good people. Our people. Except for Phyllis, who was the outsider.

"They had an affair," I said. It was a statement of fact, not of condemnation.

"Frank loved your mother."

I laughed, less out of humor than embarrassment.

"He did. He tried to get her to leave Billy."

"Why didn't she? It was a mismatched marriage to begin with."

"Because of you, Bud. And Carl."

"What about after Billy died?"

"It was too late then."

"Why too late?"

"Bud, I've told you all I know."

The sound of the piano suddenly stopped in the middle of what sounded like a Schumann piece. "The Happy Farmer." Barbara played the notes but without much feeling. She came outside, a homely girl without any talent. I could see her following down Peggy's path.

"Hi, Uncle Bud," Barbara said. Peggy had bestowed this title on me, too. It was her way of keeping her past intact. She put her arm around her daughter's shoulders.

I got on my bike.

"Mary Russell knew Frank as well as anyone around here," Peggy said. "I'm surprised you haven't talked to her." I had the feeling this was for Barbara's benefit, letting her know the gist of her mother's conversation with me.

"Thanks," I said. "I'll do that."

"You playing tomorrow night at the benefit, Uncle Bud?"

"Yes, I'm the warm-up act for the Subsonics." A local rock group that I'm sure Barbara was more interested in than me.

As I biked away, Peggy and Barbara both waved, then turned and walked back to the house arm in arm.

53

Key West had always served as a kind of hideout for drifters. Something about being out in the ocean a hundred miles from the mainland, away from America, gave people the belief they could escape. Key West was like a foreign country in many ways. Draft dodgers showed up here in the sixties; guys hiding from the IRS, the FBI, the DEA, and the WPA—wives pursuing alimony. At one time work was available on fishing boats and in the tourist joints that paid off the books, and a person could live in a shack or under a tree someplace, no questions asked.

It was a place in which to get lost. Except that everybody in town knew everybody else's dirty little secret. It wouldn't leave the rock, but the price of protection was the knowledge that everybody in Key West knew your business.

As a community we could be as hardheaded about protecting our own people's secrets as we were loose in revealing those of the strangers among us.

The missing connection between the Bayards and Lila Murphy, was, I was sure, Frank Paine. Titus Walker intimated as much when I went to see him. Someone knew what Frank had done, and why, and it was that information I sought.

I mentioned it to Casey over dinner.

"Didn't you know him?" she asked. Meaning Frank. "I thought it was such a small town in those days that everybody knew everybody."

"I knew him, but he was part of my parents' generation and I wasn't privy to the dirt. Also, that was the time when I was in Korea."

"Was there any dirt?"

"You mean besides Phyllis?" I had told Casey everything. "As far as I know, Frank had a reputation as a ladies' man. That's all. He was well respected otherwise, a good sheriff."

"Could he have been involved with the Murphy girl?"

"I don't think so." It had occurred to me, but if he was, then where did the Bayards come into it? Somehow it just didn't fit. I believed Peggy when she said that Frank Paine had been in love with Phyllis. Peggy might have been boring, but she got the details right.

"What do you remember about him?"

"Frank?"

Casey nodded.

Frank Paine. He always wore a tie, I remembered. Not like the lawyers along Whitehead Street, the Farquars who pranced around looking uncomfortable in their suits; Frank wore a tie the way a cook wore an apron, almost like it was molded onto him. Never a jacket. The sleeves of his shirt were always rolled up to his elbows, and when he was on the streets, he had on a wide-brimmed straw hat. There was something casual yet at the same time elegant about him. It was easy to see how women would have been attracted to him.

There was nothing phony or high-hat about Frank either. He would go into the dingiest bars and buy a round, chat with people, just sort of keeping in touch. I think he probably had good cop instincts. I'd see him around the Garden of Palms once in a while and we would speak, but we never had any sustained conversations that I can remember.

It was in the Garden of Palms that I busted someone's head one night—I don't even remember whose now—for hinting at a relationship between Frank and Phyllis. Now I can see why Frank would have kept his distance from me. Whatever was going on between him and Phyllis, he wouldn't have wanted to make it appear that I was somehow party to it.

He was a tall, angular guy with thick brown hair swept back from a widow's peak on his high forehead. He was a heavy smoker, Frank, and a guy who volunteered his time and the resources from the Monroe County Sheriff's Department to aid in various community projects throughout the year. I assumed he owed political patronage to the Bayards since nearly everyone in those years in any position of authority down here did.

That was the extent of my knowledge of Frank Paine, I told Casey. We had finished eating. I was still hungry. I suggested we walk up the street to an ice cream emporium and get a couple of cones, or better yet, a quart and take it back to the house.

"A sweet tooth, huh?" Casey smiled knowingly.

At home, I spooned vanilla into two bowls, lacing it with liquid chocolate, and took them out on the front porch where Casey sat in the swing. I sat next to her and we ate our ice cream watching the light flow of traffic along Duval in June. The air was still, but the humidity was up and I felt a trickle of sweat run down the middle of my back.

We were quiet, eating our ice cream, absorbed in our own thoughts, with the occasional clink of our spoons against the glass bowls. Finally I said, "Do you want to talk about it?"

"I'm not sure."

"I need to know."

We finished the ice cream and sat holding the empty bowls. When she spoke, Casey didn't look at me. We both sat staring straight ahead.

"Alex was curious about you. He asked a lot of questions. I didn't think anything of it until I came up to the Club that night and you told me."

I didn't say anything. I knew she would tell me, or not tell me, but my asking her questions wasn't going to make it any easier.

"He wanted to know what you'd told me about New Orleans, what had happened there. It was always very casual, you know, he never pressed me."

No, of course, that wasn't Farquar's style. He was insidious. I felt a loathing for him I hadn't anticipated.

"Then I found him going through some of my stuff one time. It was no big deal, there was nothing there, it was just odd."

"Did you confront him?"

"No. I've just never seen him again."

We sat there for another half hour, mostly in silence. Finally, we went inside. Tom came out and Casey knelt on the floor in my office to scratch his ears. I put a George

Shearing tape in the cassette player I had in the kitchen and started to wash up the empty bowls I'd carried in.

When Casey came in, she put her arms around me from behind as I stood at the sink.

"You want anything?" I asked.

"No. I'm tired."

We went to bed, but the sheets were damp and smelled of mildew and our previous coupling. We lay on our backs without touching. I must have fallen asleep because when I woke, she was sitting on the edge of the bed. The George Shearing tape was still playing. I could hear Casey crying softly. I put out my hand and touched her bare back.

"I'll be okay," she said.

"I know."

The next morning when I woke up, she was gone.

"Frank Paine," Mary Russell said, shaking her head. "A good man. The best." She sat behind a desk that was buried beneath scraps of papers and clippings in the research section of the library. "Bud, I haven't seen you in a couple of weeks. I thought you'd gotten this out of your system. Still pursuing that ancient murder case?"

"I am. Frank Paine was the sheriff at the time."

"Yes, he was. We could use more like him."

Mary seemed to be breathing better, there was less wheezing, and she could talk without a coughing attack every other word.

"Mary, you sound better. What have you been doing?"

She smiled. "Yoga."

"What?"

"I'm doing yoga."

"Come on! Where you get into those contortions?"

"There's nothing wrong with my muscles, you old fool. It's my lungs that are bad, and believe it or not after all these years I'm getting some relief."

I rolled my eyes, trying to picture her with her legs wrapped behind her head, not a pretty picture. She swatted at me with a rolled newspaper. "You ought to try it. Might loosen you up a little."

"I'll keep it in mind," I said. "What can you tell me about Frank Paine besides what a nice guy he was?"

"What do you want to know?" While we talked, Mary never stopped sifting through papers on her desk, banding some of them together, occasionally pausing to look more attentively at one yellowing historical document or another.

"For starters, what was his relationship to the Bayards?"

Mary looked at me blankly. "I suppose he knew them, like everybody else in town. What kind of a question is that?"

"I mean, was he beholden to them in any way?"

Mary laughed. "For his position, you mean? Politically?"

I nodded.

"As far as I know, absolutely not."

"He wasn't John T.'s man?"

"He wasn't anyone's man."

I was set back momentarily. It must have shown on my face because Mary said, "What's the matter, Bud? This doesn't suit your needs in your war against the Bayards?"

I was beginning to feel foolish. Everyone in town it seemed saw me as a thorn in the side of the Bayards. "I just thought everybody who got elected back then was probably part of the Bayard machine."

Mary waved her hand in front of her face. "Pshaa. Just talk. Frank Paine had a pretty solid political base of his own. Now that's not to say there was any great animosity between the Bayards and Frank because I don't think there was."

"So he might have had Bayard support without owing them anything."

"Possible. Look it up. See who ran against him for sheriff. Offhand I can't recall."

"I'll do that," I said. "Frank was quite a ladies' man, wasn't he?"

Mary chuckled. "Oh, you guys are all alike as far as I'm concerned. Frank wasn't any worse than the next one."

"What's the worst thing you could say about him?"

"I try not to speak ill of the dead." Mary laughed. "The worst fault Frank Paine had he was too easygoing. People took advantage of him. He was a good administrator, a good sheriff, but he was a sucker for a sob story."

"A dangerous habit for a lawman, wasn't it?"

"Oh, Frank made some blunders, sure. But he also helped a lot of people. Invested in them."

"In what way?"

"Well, there were a couple of guys he got out of jail, released to his custody, and found jobs for them, one I still see around today. Stuff you couldn't do now with all the red tape. But it was easy back then when one man had some control."

"You mean he let people off?"

"Oh, Bud, you know what I'm talking about. Frank

just had a good sense of character, what would work with people."

"And sometimes it didn't."

"Sometimes. Now look up who he ran against and let me get some work done."

It took half an hour but I found it on the fiche, articles from the local paper covering the three consecutive elections Frank had won. His opponents were small potatoes, or unknown names all together. Not Bayard people, Mary confirmed.

"Whatever happened to Frank?" I asked her.

"Joined the Conch exodus to Ocala and lived up there on a horse farm until he died."

"Never married?"

"Nope."

If Mary Russell knew—and I assumed she did—about Frank's relationship with Phyllis, she didn't give me any indication of it. I thanked her for her help and started to leave.

"I see you're playing at the benefit tonight," Mary said.

"I am. Will you be there?"

"Wouldn't miss it."

I nodded and went out.

Frank Paine was more of an enigma than ever. Outside the purview of the Bayards, he was a man who could get prisoners released, who looked after the public weal and the racial harmony of the city by hiring a black as his second-in-command; a womanizer. Could he have been compromised somehow, either by his personal conduct or through some mistake within the judicial system?

The answer was obvious. But how did it relate to the Bayards and the death of Lila Murphy? I wondered. And more, how would I ever prove it?

From the library I biked over to the state attorney's office behind the courthouse on the chance that Alex Farquar was not in court today, and got lucky.

The receptionist buzzed him in his office and Alex came out looking sheepish.

"I need a minute of your time," I said.

"Of course, Gideon. Anytime."

I followed him back to his office. We stepped inside and he closed the door. "Now, what can I do for you?"

"I'm looking into the leak that cost a kid his life in New Orleans."

"Oh, now, Gideon—"

"I don't know where it came from, but I want you to have fair warning. There isn't an office in this building that will be outside my probe. That includes yours."

"Gideon, Gideon, Gideon."

"Forewarned is forearmed." I opened the door and stalked out. I was testing him because I had nothing to go on. If he was working both sides of the street, I reasoned, and I could provoke some fear in him, maybe he would make a move. He had everything to lose, I had everything to gain. Or so I believed at the time.

55

I decided it was time to make peace with Carl. We would be sharing a stage tonight, and I could see no reason for it to be uncomfortable for either of us. Afterward, he would return to Tallahassee, and our paths might not cross for another year. If then. I was worried about Carl, worried about his health. I hadn't liked what I saw in his demeanor the last time we were together. There were things that I wanted to resolve with him. I wasn't sure how to do that because it was so difficult to talk to Carl, to confront each other without confronting our individual memories of our past. Which meant confronting Phyllis and Captain Billy.

I had uncovered within myself a deep well of sorrow for Phyllis. Her life with Billy must have been a nightmare. Now, to know that she had turned down the lasting love she might have enjoyed with Frank Paine because of Carl and me was one of life's bitter twists. It was not for me to judge Phyllis, but despite the sorrow it somehow pleased me to know that, however briefly, she had at least had some pleasure, and who knows, perhaps even retribution for the years she had stuck to an unhappy marriage.

If Carl was unable to accept that knowledge, then it seemed to me that he would be equally unable to accept a resolution between us. Who we were was so much a part of who Phyllis was, because she more than Captain Billy had determined the course of our lives.

As I rode up to the intersection of Carl's place, I saw him come out the front door and get into a waiting cab. He didn't see me, and I waited for the cab to drive away and then on impulse pedaled my bike after it.

If the cab stayed in old town, I could probably follow it. If it headed out toward the boulevards to the shopping plazas or the airport, I had no chance. But I was in luck; Carl was going downtown.

The cab drove up to the covered entrance of the hotel where Carl and I had had dinner the other night. I watched from behind a parked car some distance away as Carl paid the driver and went into the hotel. I looked at my watch. It was twelve-twenty. I locked my bike at a nearby rack and walked into the hotel grounds to the pool area where there was a bar from which I could watch the entrance to the restaurant.

Carl was waiting with Jack Bayard for the maître d' to seat them.

I ordered a club soda, taking five minutes to drink it before I walked over to the restaurant. It wasn't necessary to go inside to see them. Carl and Jack were seated at a table next to one of the windows overlooking the harbor. I stood on the deck outside with a view of the pool and watched them for a moment.

Carl, normally placid, was visibly upset. I had never seen him so animated. His face was red, and he gestured wildly, but apparently he was able to keep his voice under control. Jack seemed to be listening intently.

There was no way I could get inside and close enough to their table to hear without being seen. I watched as a waiter came over and took their order. Carl sat back, looking drained, his back rigid. When the waiter left, Jack spoke and seemed to calm Carl. I watched a few more minutes, then went back to the tiki bar where I ordered the cheapest sandwich on the menu. For the same cost I could have eaten for a week in the drugstore.

Around the pool people lay in deck chairs absorbing the sun, their bodies glistening with creams and lotions. A group of older women, led by a young woman counting cadence, were doing some form of exercise in the pool while a waiter in a sweat-stained white shirt carried pastel-colored drinks among the sunbathers. The irritating drone of Jet Skis in the harbor mixed with the whine of a radio commercial beamed through the hotel's speaker system. What a difference twenty years could make. I never thought I would be nostalgic for the days when this area was a boatyard and the noise one heard was a pipe fitter banging out the ding in a boat's propeller.

I paid for my sandwich and soda, leaving a modest tip. It was almost one-thirty when Carl and Jack came out of the restaurant. Jack had his hand on Carl's shoulder. I waited until they'd walked back toward the hotel's reception area, then went to retrieve my bike.

In the parking lot Carl was getting into Jack's pickup truck. I trailed them down Simonton Street, thinking Jack would let Carl off at the office, but they went on, turning down Fleming to Margaret Street, where Jack took a right. At the entrance to the cemetery the truck stopped and Carl got out. Jack drove away. I was surprised when Carl walked into the cemetery.

I waited a few minutes beneath the shade of a banyan tree, then rode through the iron gates. Carl was standing before Phyllis's and Captain Billy's crypts. The purple flowers from the African orchids I'd placed at the grave the last time I was here were gone. Bare stems remained in the container.

Carl looked up when I stopped beside him, his face marked, it seemed to me, with surprise and something else, pain maybe. Or disappointment. Perhaps I hadn't given Carl enough credit and he was confronting the past.

"The odd couple," I said.

"What?"

I nodded in the direction of the crypts. "Phyllis and Captain Billy." I saw immediately it was the wrong thing to have said. "Till death do us part."

"Bud, please. Do we have to go through this?"

"No. I'm glad to see you here."

"Why? You don't think I ever come here?"

"I don't know your habits anymore. Maybe I never did."

"Because you don't have to read about them in the newspaper."

Touché. "I'm doing my best."

"Good," Carl said. "I hope you have a long and happy life."

"Likewise. And I hope we settle our differences."

Carl shook his head. There was moisture in one of his eyes. I couldn't tell if it was age or emotion. "And I hope you call off this crusade you're on. Especially now."

I knew better than to ask why because I knew the answer. Maybe I'd known it for some time. It was written all over Carl's face. But the words came out anyway. "What do you mean *now?*"

"Because, Bud," my brother, Carl, said, "I'm dying."

56

Cancer. The big C. The Lowry curse, and Carl had it. Leukemia just like Captain Billy's. Six months to live, he told me. No more. So it wasn't just a family visit he was making. Carl was here taking some final inventory.

"Why didn't you tell me sooner?" I felt angry, cheated in a way for never having been a participant in the life of my own kin.

Carl shrugged. "You seemed preoccupied with your own problems."

I laughed nervously. "I'm sorry." I meant it. I was sorry for the gulf that separated us. I didn't know what to say. Peggy would have known what to do, she would have been able to bridge that gulf. She would have brought Carl home, fixed a big meal, chattered away endlessly making plans for one thing or another, while

Carl and I sat stiffly around the table. But I wasn't married to Peggy anymore.

"We're all sorry," Carl said. "Life never turns out the way you plan it." He had changed. All that anger I'd seen in the restaurant earlier was gone. He seemed somehow resigned to his fate.

"How long have you known?"

"I stopped in Miami before I came down here to have some tests done. I just got the results the other day."

"They can't do anything?"

"Too far advanced."

I felt the rising heat from the asphalt penetrate the soles of my shoes. The long boat oar that the green sailor was holding as he stood vigil over the Spanish-American War dead stretched upward toward a billowing cloud formation just overhead that was like an explosion. The lower edges of the clouds were gunmetal gray, bunching up into feathery whiteness.

"What are you going to do?"

"Spend a few more days here putting things in order. Then I'll return to Tallahassee."

I knew Carl would have everything planned out to the last detail. He would leave nothing to chance. Where he would be hospitalized; who would look after him. The details of his funeral.

"What can I do?"

Carl shook his head. "Call off your war against Jack Bayard. Stop fighting them."

Carl the peacemaker, the elder statesman. My brother's dying request.

I nodded. "You don't want to know where this investigation is going?"

"No. I already know more than I want to know. I've watched this for too many years. Honor me."

It was vintage Carl, wanting me to honor him. I suppose it was the best that I could expect in the way of reconciliation. Don't try to bridge the gulf. Just honor me, your older brother.

"I would like to spend some time with you," I said. "Before you go back. I'm trying to absorb this. There are things we're going to need to talk about."

"When? I'm pretty busy."

"How about tomorrow evening?"

Carl seemed to think for a moment. "I've got dinner plans, but the early evening is free. Come by then."

I got on the bike and started to turn around. "By the way," Carl said, "I'm not advertising my condition."

Of course. I went back out through the chain-link gates I'd come in. When I turned to look back, Carl was leaning against the white cement crypts, his tall, thin frame stooped. I thought I saw his back contort as though a sob had escaped him. Probably I was mistaken. I'd never seen Carl break down before, not even as a kid during the sick years. There had always been some stoic rigidity about him, some level determination, a defiance of pain and adversity.

For some reason I thought of the year he graduated from high school, the yearbook he carried home to Phyllis. Almost every handwritten entry had some form of the observation that Carl was the most likely to succeed. I wonder if he felt he had fulfilled all those expectations.

At home I was not surprised to find a message to call Ray Welch, the state attorney.

"Gideon," Ray said when I got him on the line, "what's this I hear from my man Farquar that you're launching some kind of an independent investigation."

I chuckled softly. Alex must have been quaking. "Don't worry about it, Ray. This is between me and Alex."

"What do you mean don't worry about it? I run this

place. If there's something going on I don't know about, tell me."

"I'm surprised Alex didn't tell you."

"Something about your not being happy with the way things turned out in New Orleans."

"You're damned right I wasn't happy. A man I was supposed to have been protecting got killed."

"And you're blaming this office?"

"I'm raising questions. Alex told me he'd already conducted an inquiry. You didn't know about this?"

"Only vaguely. But you can be sure I'll look into it now."

"Appreciate that, Ray."

"Just do me a favor."

"What's that?"

"Don't go off half-cocked on this one."

I hung up and walked down to the garage to pick up the Buick. After I'd paid the bill a kid brought my car around and got out, holding the door for me. "Beautiful day, isn't it, Mr. Lowry?" he said.

"Just beautiful," I said. "Just beautiful."

57

The benefit was held each year in the brick Civil War fortress across from the ocean near the airport. The fort itself housed a museum devoted to Keys' history that contained a dusty display of the relics of my people.

It was early evening when I drove out South Roosevelt Boulevard past the town houses and the row of tall palms, their trunks forever curved landward like crooked spines, bent by the wind sweeping off the ocean. I parked near the fort and went in to check the equipment and make sure everything was ready to go when Harry and I went onstage at seven. We only had to play a couple of hours before the speeches and the raffle began. Afterward the Subsonics would come on and rock through the night.

Food caterers were setting up their stands around the interior perimeter of the octagonal fort, and three service bars were already in place with rows of cloth-draped tables filled with generic booze and mixers.

Colored lanterns were strung around the walls of the fort and through some of the palm trees. The platform stage had been put up near the center of the grassy open-air quadrangle, with the brick lookout tower as a backdrop. A couple of audio guys were going through the ritual testing, testing, testing procedure in front of the microphone.

I joined them on the stage. The piano was an upright with the facing removed to expose the hammers and strings. A microphone was angled down near the soundboard. I nodded to the technicians and stood in front of the piano and picked out the base rhythm of a boogie-woogie with my left hand.

"Hey, all right!" one of the guys working with the mikes said.

Moments later Harry came in with his guitar. He came up onstage, plugged into the amplifying equipment, adjusted the volume, and when he was ready, I gave him some chords to tune up to.

Later, we went down to one of the bars together and I got a Coca-Cola. Harry had a beer. A few people were beginning to arrive. We wandered around the grounds with our drinks.

At a Mexican food stand there were some burritos ready, and Harry and I each ate one. "I was talking to Ronnie the other day," Harry said.

"That's all you were doing with her, talking?"

"Hey, she's a nice girl."

"When did you begin discriminating?"

Harry grinned. "She says the management at the Club's thinking of laying us off for the summer if business doesn't pick up."

I wasn't surprised. "What'll you do?"

"Maybe go north for a couple months." Harry was from Minnesota. "What about you?"

"Tough it out." I had no north to go to. This was it.

One of the organizers came by. "You guys about ready to go on?" he asked.

"Anytime," I said.

"Well, then, let's rock and roll."

Harry and I finished our burritos and walked back around to the stage. A couple of spotlights had been turned on. Overhead the evening light was fading as the colored lanterns began to shed light. I could smell the sea, mixed with cooking spices from the food stands, and there was the insistent hum of people as the crowd increased.

"E-flat," I said, sitting down to the piano. " 'I've Got You Under My Skin.' "

"Ouch, that hurts," Harry said.

I touched the keys. *Ba bah bah ba bah ba bah.* We were on our way. Waking up to reality.

Reality was a killer. It was cancer. Murder. It took some people and left others, the Virginia Murphys and Karen Barlows, to make sense of it all, altering lives in ways that could never be put back together. Reality. Who needs it? Reality was something to escape from, and I had been running from it all my life. I should have known that it would catch me sooner or later, that I would have to deal with Captain Billy, and now Carl.

"Play it, Bud," someone shouted from the crowd.

I looked down into a sea of faces, smiled, nodded in the direction of the voice while continuing to play, giving Harry the key changes and flowing from one piece to another. Once in a while people applauded, whistled, pausing to listen for a moment before they moved on.

We played for an hour, then took a break. I went to take a leak and, coming out of the john, ran into Webb Conners, who was in uniform, part of security.

"Sounding good up there, Bud," Webb said. "Been a while since I've heard you play."

"Thanks," I said. "You come up with anything for me?"

"What? On that phone call? Bud, it's only been a couple of days."

"Just wondering."

Webb hooked his thumbs into the black leather holster belt that held his gear. "I've tried." Webb glanced around him. People were moving past us, talking, laughing, while someone onstage pitched raffle tickets over the loudspeaker system. "If anyone knows anything, they're holding on to it. I'm not sure I can do any more without creating suspicion."

"All right, Webb. I appreciate it." I started to turn away.

Webb stopped me. "You understand, don't you, Bud?"

"I understand. Don't worry about it."

I went back up onstage. We played for another hour, and when we were done, I milled around the crowd, pausing here and there to speak to people I knew. I would have left if Carl weren't speaking, but I wanted to hear him. While standing in line for another Coke, I felt a tug on my shirt. I turned and saw Casey. She gave me her wave.

"You want something?" I asked.

"The usual."

I got her a club soda and we found an out-of-the-way corner up against the building where we could sit without being trampled. "Your brother doesn't look so good," Casey said.

Carl was taking his place up onstage. Folding chairs had been set up in front of the piano and amplifying equipment. Carl sat between the Key West mayor and the county mayor. The three of them talked back and forth, Carl telling them a story, talking the way he did when he was on public display. No, he didn't look good under the light. There were deep shadows under his eyes and in the hollows of his cheeks. I was surprised he hadn't worn makeup.

A spokesperson, a woman I didn't know, went to the microphone and announced that Portia Villani had left the hospital today, and that this particular benefit was a special tribute to her on behalf of all the years she had worked and contributed to its success. She called for a round of applause. Half the people here probably didn't even know who Portia Villani was.

Afterward the county mayor spoke, then Key West's mayor, who introduced Carl Lowry, a man who needed no introduction, the mayor said, because he'd been around so long. Polite laughter. Scattered applause.

Carl stood up and put his notes on the lectern, made a show of putting on his glasses, then held up his hands to stop the applause, which was really very limited. Perhaps he sensed that the crowd was simply enduring one more political speech before the boat was raffled.

Carl began with a joke about his longevity in the Senate, joking that he would try to keep the speech somewhat shorter.

It struck me then that this could possibly be the last speech Carl would make as a politician. And he knew it.

58

The speech. I would forever remember it in just that way: the speech. It was over in fifteen minutes, or less. Eloquent, witty, and substantive. All of the things I was unaccustomed to hearing from a speech by Senator Carl Lowry. It was also a political departure, a hundred and eighty degrees away from the philosophy I had associated with Carl all these years.

I looked around the crowd, trying to gauge its reaction, to see if anyone else was as surprised as I was, but there was nothing but silence. People listened as Carl talked about our heritage here, the fragility of our resources, the absolute need to control growth in order to save a system that would be crucial, not just to future generations of Keys' residents, but to the entire planet. He brought it down to a personal level by talking about his father, Captain Billy, and the difference a few generations had made to life on and in the sea. He talked about Phyllis.

It was not just an environmental speech (John T. Bayard would have called it a Commie speech), it was an emotional, personal reflection. And I think when he was done, people recognized that. There was a moment's hesitation before anyone applauded.

I was astounded. I remembered how angry Carl had seemed when he was with Jack Bayard earlier, and I wondered if he'd been making his break from their camp at that time.

I applauded along with everyone else. I felt a bonding, a sense of renewal with this man who had been an enigma for so many years; a brother in name only. There was definitely a momentous sense of pride, of . . . family. Hope wasn't a natural part of my nature, but I saw a homecoming of sorts even if it was to be short-lived. Perhaps I was wrong. Perhaps it was all theater, but I didn't want to believe so.

Casey squeezed my hand as we stood up. I watched Carl tuck his glasses away and drop the notes he had barely used into his shirt pocket as he sat back down without expression.

I looked for the Bayards in the crowd but didn't see them. I did see Peggy, who stood with Jake and Barbara at the edge of the stage. I saw Webb standing in front of the exit doors, his arms crossed over his broad chest. Standing there chewing gum he seemed oblivious to what had just happened. I saw Judge Watson, who stood apart from the crowd, leaning against a palm tree.

As people began to move around, I recognized some of the courthouse cronies and people from the state attorney's office. I didn't see Alex Farquar.

"I want to talk to Carl before he leaves," I said to Casey. I was sure he wouldn't hang around; he had made his statement and he would not want to talk about it.

Casey smiled and released my hand.

I started toward the stage as the officials were coming down, but the crowd was too dense to get through it quickly. People were clapping me on the back. "Bud, that was some speech," someone said as though it were mine. I looked around, but whoever had spoken was swept away in the surge of the crowd. I tried to muscle my way to the outside where I'd seen Peggy earlier. I could see the top of Carl's head disappearing down the opposite side of the stage twenty yards away and knew I could never get to him before he left.

By the time I got free, the boat raffle was beginning and access to the stage was cut off once again. I started back in the opposite direction, thinking I might be able to intercept Carl by going around the back, but there were long lines at the bars and food stands, with people blocking the pathways.

"Doesn't this kind of remind you of the Garden of Palms, Bud?"

I recognized Mary Russell's voice before I saw her. She was standing a few feet away balancing a paper plate of rice and beans and a plastic drink cup.

"What? You mean the lanterns?"

"Well, that and seeing so many old-timers congregated in one place, partying. Kind of a shocker of a speech, huh? Coming from Carl."

"He's full of surprises," I said. "Have you seen him come around here."

"Nope. You'll find him though. I'm glad to see you two getting together."

I kept working my way around and saw George Lewis looking straight at me as he came from the opposite direction.

"Bud, good to see you. Let me buy you a drink."

"I gave it up," I said.

"Come on, I don't believe it. You're such a grand guy when you've had a couple." He laughed. "Loosen you up a little."

"You didn't tell me about the phone call," I said.

"What phone call?"

"The one that came in to Virginia Murphy the night she died."

George looked as if a bad taste had just come into his mouth from the pit of his stomach. He tried to smile. "Bud, you never give up, do you? I thought you'd done with this."

"Did you send those two tough guys out to question Jack?"

"Bud, let's have a drink. You want to talk about this, come by the office." He caught my arm at the elbow, trying to be chummy. I pulled away from him. "All right, Bud. You're going to be that way." George threw up his hands and walked away. I wondered how long it would take him before he called Jack Bayard.

I found Webb standing guard at the doors. "You see Carl?"

"You just missed him. He left a few minutes ago."

Casey was talking to Peggy and Jake Maloney. As I approached them, I overheard Peggy say, "The two of them have never been close."

"Speak of the devil," Jake said.

"Oh, Bud," Peggy said. "I saw you earlier with this girl"—she seemed to put some emphasis on *girl,* and I saw Casey grimace—"and I wanted to meet her."

That was just like Peggy. She would come out of nowhere and tell a total stranger her life story. She was banal, but well-meaning. Of course I had told her about

Casey, but this was the first time they'd met. I shook hands with Jake.

"I was telling Casey how you and Carl have never really been close."

"Now, Peg," Jake said. "Maybe that's not your place."

Peggy looked hurt.

"It's all right," I said. "Casey knows about Carl and me."

"Wasn't that a fabulous speech, Bud?" Peggy said. Nothing could keep Peggy's mood down for long. "I was so proud of him, the things he said about Billy and Phyllis."

Jake seemed embarrassed.

"It was a good speech." I took Casey's hand.

Peggy smiled at us. "Well, it was lovely meeting you," she said, extending her hand to Casey.

"You, too," Casey said.

They were about to walk away when Barbara wandered over and Peggy introduced her to Casey. Barbara looked bored. She looked like a lonely child. Once again I thanked whatever conjunction of stars occurred that I wasn't standing in Jake's shoes today.

"She's nice, but I can't believe you were married to her," Casey said when we were alone.

"I can't believe it either at times, except that Conch boys tend to settle for what's safe."

"Was Carl ever married?"

"No," I said. "I used to wonder about that. Now I think he just spent so much time alone because he was sick when he was growing up that he never learned how to interact with women."

Casey seemed to find that hard to believe. "Doesn't he even have a companion, or anything?"

"I don't know what he does in Tallahassee, but I've never known him to be out with a woman here."

She shook her head. The Subsonics were beginning to tune up. "Shall we get out of here?" I asked.

Casey agreed and we headed to the parking lot. We both had our cars. I walked with Casey to hers and stood with her for a moment while she unlocked the door and got in. "If you feel like coming over, Bud, you can. I've got some work I've got to do, but it won't take more than an hour."

I thought about it. I was feeling restive and I wanted to talk about Carl and the speech and his situation. I realized I might also be afraid I was going to have another urge to drink, and I didn't want to be alone. "Yes," I said. "I'll meet you over there."

I closed her door and was walking to my car when I saw the judge wending his way through parked cars as I reached the Buick. "Bud." He came over and we stood leaning against the Buick's fender. "Your boy's coming to court tomorrow in the Cleansweep trial."

"Farquar?"

Watson nodded. "I wouldn't be surprised if we wound up with a mistrial."

I told Just about my visit to Farquar the other day and the phone call from Ray Welch. "Well, you probably did the right thing," he said. "Take the ball to them."

"What I've probably done is put myself out of work."

"I'll speak to Ray for you if you like."

"No, I'm going to let it ride for a while, see what happens."

Just took a cigar from his pocket and rolled it around in his mouth without lighting it. I opened the car door and yellow light leaked out on the ground, which I noticed was littered with cigarette butts. "Quite a speech by Carl tonight," the judge said.

"Everybody is talking about it."

"What's gotten into him?"

I wanted to say cancer, but I had promised Carl I wouldn't tell anyone. I knew that with Casey I would break that promise, but I was sure she would not talk about it. I slid behind the wheel and turned the key in the ignition. The big V-8 turned over at once, purring restlessly after its tune-up.

"Bud, don't worry about anything. You get in a jam, I can always help you out."

"Thanks. I'll be okay."

Just stepped back from the car and I put it in gear. As I drove out of the lot, I could hear the Subsonics wailing into the night.

It was almost ten o'clock by the time I got to Casey's. The light was on in the front room, which she'd made into a study. The house itself was a shotgun, small, with the study, then a bath and bedroom off a straight hallway that led back to the kitchen and living room. The floors and walls were all bare wood.

Casey let me in, said she would be just a few more minutes, to make myself comfortable, then disappeared back into the study. I walked back to the living area and stretched out on the couch beneath the ceiling fan.

Casey paid no particular attention to domestic details. A few haphazard pieces of furniture, a lot of paperback books scattered around, papers piled on a table, a couple of filing cabinets shoved against a wall that held some of her drawings.

"Troubled?"

I must have dozed. I was startled awake by her voice behind me. "Sorry," she said. "I didn't know you were asleep. You were mumbling." I sat up on the couch. Casey sat next to it on the floor, tucking a long nightshirt she'd put on down between her knees.

"Ah, I don't know," I said.

"Talk about it?"

I talked about my youth, what it was like growing up in the house on William Street. I talked about Carl. I tried to describe my feelings tonight at the benefit. It wasn't easy. I was troubled. I was troubled by Lila Murphy, whose smiling face now haunted my dreams.

"What happens to us?" I asked Casey.

She smiled. "One day at a time."

A day at a time. It made everything sound so easy. I was already thinking about tomorrow and what I was going to say to Carl when we had our first and maybe our last real conversation.

How do, Bud." Sweetwater was sitting at his usual place at the counter when I went into the drugstore for breakfast the next morning on my way home from Casey's.

Putting an extra spoonful of sugar in my coffee when the waitress brought it, I glanced at the front page of the morning *Herald* beside me on the counter. The usual sorrowful news. How easy it was, I thought, to read this stuff day in and day out without remembering most of it for more than a few hours. And yet it gradually changed our lives as each of these stories became a statistic. The accumulation of despair, and one day we're locking doors that had once been left open, and buying guns to protect ourselves.

Lila Murphy was part of those statistics, that accumulation. Yet, like so many others, Lila Murphy was forgotten.

I looked at Sweets's face across the counter. The folds of flesh just below his cheekbones that were like vertical seams down to his jaw.

We didn't forget, I thought, we just tucked this stuff away where it wouldn't interfere with our lives. But in a face like Sweetwater's you could see it all stored in there, banded, leaving creases like the metal strapping on wooden crates.

I ate my breakfast and walked home, leaving the Buick parked where it was as close probably as I was going to get it to my house.

I opened the front door and stepped inside, then slowly closed the door and stood with my back against it.

My place had been ransacked. Tossed, literally, as if stuff had been picked up and flung into the air. Chairs tipped over, desk drawers emptied on the floor, the pictures of Phyllis and Captain Billy askew on the walls. I listened. There were no sounds except the hum of the laboring refrigerator motor from the kitchen. I walked in there and found equal destruction. The refrigerator door was standing open, the table tipped over with utensils, appliances, and food strewn everywhere. Tom's food and water bowl were tipped over, water streaks across the floor.

In the bathroom the medicine chest was open and bottles of over-the-counter stuff and ancient prescriptions had been tumbled into the sink, pills spilled across the floor. Nothing was spared. A box of Kleenex had been emptied, the roll of toilet paper removed from its holder, and the lid to the water tank on the toilet lay across the seat. Whoever had tossed the place was thorough. I took a deep breath before going into the bedroom.

My clothes were scattered, the bed stripped, and sheet

music plastered the floor, jumbled tunes staring up at me in some weirdly visual dissonance.

Virginia Murphy was a heap of ash tipped in a flattened pile on a sheet music copy of "After You've Gone," a clear footprint in the middle of the gray and gritty remains. I got down on my knees and examined the print. I guessed the intruder had stepped in the spilled water in the kitchen before coming in here. The print looked salvageable. While on the floor, I found Lila Murphy's photo facedown, caught under one leg of the piano stool.

I tiptoed back to the office, without touching anything, trying not to disturb the disorder, picked the phone up off the floor, and called George Lewis.

"Your place was what? Trashed? A guy like you, I can't believe it. What did they take?"

"I haven't done a close check. Maybe nothing."

"Well, what would you like me to do?"

"I don't know. In the old days we'd send someone around to investigate. You doing things differently today?"

"Hey, I'll send a couple my best guys right over."

When I hung up, I looked around for Tom. His bed, a couple of old T-shirts I'd thrown in the bottom of the desk drawer, unceremoniously littered the floor. I went out on the back porch and called him.

The construction was in full swing. Two Bayard dump trucks growled beyond the fence. I searched for my spare key in the moss surrounding the potted bromeliad, careful to avoid the prickly spines. The key was gone.

I went back inside and sat down in the swivel chair amidst the ruins. It could have been kids, crackheads in need of quick cash. But I knew most of the kids around here, and more importantly they knew me. This wasn't a house to break into for something to steal that could be turned quickly to cash.

Looking around, I got the feeling that the whole thing had been set up, staged. Whoever had been in here must have been looking for something specific and trashed the place to cover their tracks.

I began taking it in, bit by bit. Papers from my files were thrown around the office like so much confetti, the files themselves tipped out of the desk drawers. Tax files, correspondence, ancient cases, and case reports for the investigations I'd done for various state agencies over the years, including the state attorney's office. Most of it stuff that could have been thrown away and now would be. If nothing else, this would lead to a good housecleaning.

Down on my hands and knees I started picking through the files, matching papers to file folders. I found five of the file folders marked SA with yearly dates, some of those dates crossed out and the new year written in, going back more than ten years. I found some corresponding papers from those files, but nothing for the past year. There were other papers missing, too, but I guessed that would have been a smoke screen. I was ready to bet that whoever had been in here wanted to know what I had in my files on Operation Cleansweep.

It would take a few hours to go through it all, but I was sure I wasn't going to find anything else that was missing. I sat back down at the desk and called Casey at work, telling her what had happened.

"Oh, Bud, that's awful. Who would have done it?" she asked, then repeated herself, her voice rising in pitch. "Who?"

"I'm curious. Did Farquar know you were feeding Tom while I was in New Orleans?"

I heard her sudden intake of breath, a short gasp on

the other end of the line. "Oh, no. Oh, Bud, I'm so sorry."

"Did he?"

"God, I think so. I think I probably mentioned it. That was when he was asking questions."

"Did he know about the key?"

She hesitated. "I don't think so. I wouldn't have told him about that."

But, of course, he could have followed her here or had her followed.

"Bud, I'll come over and help you clean up."

"Don't worry about it."

"I want to."

"Not necessary. Anyway, I've got the police coming over." In fact they were at the door. I hung up and let in the same two detectives who had been here the day I'd heard of Virginia's death. They took a look around and Blondie made a hissing sound through his teeth. Longhair didn't look happy to see me.

"You find anything missing?" Blondie asked.

"No, but I did find a footprint." At this point I didn't choose to mention the missing files. I didn't think it wise to point a finger at the state attorney's office right now.

I took them into the bedroom.

"What is that?" Longhair was on the floor, his nose six inches from the ashes.

"Crematory remains," I said.

"Cream what?"

"Ashes."

"Fried body parts," Blondie added.

"Oh, Jesus, man!" Longhair stood up.

"Don't worry, she's dead, she won't bite." I left them to take their plaster cast, or whatever they did these days, and went to the office to begin cleaning up.

When the cops were done, they came out and asked some questions, filling out a report, then left. I went into the bedroom and reboxed what was left of Virginia Murphy.

61

By noon I had some order restored when Tom wandered in through the hole in the back door like an actor responding to his cue. He ate, then preened himself in the middle of the kitchen floor before climbing into the desk drawer as if nothing had ever been amiss.

I sat down at the desk and called Bayard Cement. Jack's secretary told me he was in town today. She said that she thought he would be at the city building after lunch. I ate a couple of bananas and some peanut butter spread on soda crackers and, a little after one o'clock, rode my bike over to the city parking garage.

Jack's pickup truck was there, on the ground floor of the two-story garage, parked at a meter that had less than an hour on it. I locked my bike along the rail embedded in a retaining wall and went inside the city building upstairs to George Lewis's office. I half expected to find Jack there.

"What do you want?" George asked.

I stood in the open door. "Your boys tell you they got a foot impression from my place?"

"Yeah, they told me. Now what do you propose we do with it, go door-to-door checking everyone's footwear?"

"I'd narrow it down to the Cleansweep defendants and their associates."

George looked at me in disbelief. "Where do you come up with this stuff, Bud?"

"Detective work. You should try it sometime." I stepped back and closed the door.

Downstairs I saw Jack through the glass door of the city's finance department. I waited in the hallway for him to come out. When he glanced my way, he appeared to be about to wave, as if he wasn't sure at first who I was, then turned back to the counter where he was doing business. When he came out of the office, he avoided eye contact. I followed him out to the parking garage.

"I didn't see you at the benefit last night," I said.

Jack unlocked the cab door to the pickup. I noticed he still wore his high school graduation ring on his right ring finger.

"You missed one hell of a speech," I said. "Kind of a departure from his usual stuff. You might have found it interesting."

"Bud, what have you got on your mind? You didn't follow me out here to talk about your brother's speech."

"Well, now that you mention it, I wanted to ask you about that phone call you made to Virginia Murphy the night she died."

Jack had one foot on the cab's gleaming steel running board, his back to me, about to get into the truck. His shoulders slumped noticeably as he turned around, holding the door open with one hand, but the expression in his eyes was pure anger.

"Bud, I've been through this with the police. Whether you believe it or not, they did their job. I don't have to tell you a damn thing. But just to get you off my back, and I mean this, Bud, this is it. I have any more hassles with you and there's going to be trouble."

"Why'd you call her?"

"She called me. I was returning her call. I never spoke to her."

"Was George Lewis happy with that explanation?"

"I guess he was."

"I'm a little curious why Virginia would have been calling you."

Jack's face flushed. "The same damn reason you are, Bud. She was asking questions from forty years back. Just like you."

"You knew Virginia back then?"

"No, not to speak of."

"But you did know her sister?"

"We've been through this, Bud." Jack climbed into the cab, and I put my hand on the door handle, keeping the door open.

"Knew her well enough to stir you up. And maybe Virginia remembered seeing the two of you together."

"Bud, I've given you fair warning." He rolled the window down and tried to pull the door closed. I resisted.

"What about John T.?"

Jack's eyes narrowed. "What about him?"

"How well did he know Lila?"

For a few brief seconds we were frozen in time. I saw Jack's face the way he was in high school. All the youth and innocence and recklessness revealed itself in the look he gave me, knowing he had to defend his family name. We were like two kids on the schoolyard again, and I saw it coming just in the nick of time. I stepped sideways as Jack flung open the truck door.

The edge of the door scraped my khakis, just missing my kneecap, and banging against my left wrist. I was off balance when Jack came out of the truck, his fists cocked. He caught me with a right to the belly that convinced me of just how badly out of shape I was. A taste of bile came into my mouth as I danced away, trying to regain my balance.

Jack had a year or two on me and certainly was in better shape. I couldn't even remember when I'd last been in a fight, but the instincts were still there as he weighed in. I feinted, dropping my left shoulder and coming up inside Jack's punch with a right of my own that glanced off his nose. I felt his flesh yield and danced back, seeing a trickle of blood start down his upper lip.

My fist ached; I wasn't going to be at the Club tonight playing piano.

Jack wiped his forearm across his face and came back at me. He pushed two quick jabs at me that I fielded by covering my face with both fists. In the instant that I was blinded, he slugged me again with another right to the belly that dropped me to the ground. Grit embedded itself in the heel of my palms as I broke my fall to the concrete. Bayard concrete, I thought, seeing his steel-capped boots advancing. Winded, feeling like I was going to puke, I pushed myself up on one knee.

A car turned into the parking lot from the street and Jack stepped back. I got to my feet, heaving for breath, relieved to see that Jack, too, seemed to be short of breath.

As the car went slowly past, its windows up, the occupants stared at us in disbelief. When it was gone, we came back at each other, Jack throwing roundhouses that bounced off my shoulders and forearms.

"Hey, break it up!" A couple of cops came out of the city building, running through the parking garage. They each grabbed one of us by the arms. "What the hell are you two old duffers doing?"

Duffers. I didn't know the two uniformed cops, and apparently neither did Jack. I shrugged out of the cop's grip and went over and sat on the retaining wall next to my bike.

The other cop released his hold on Jack. "Is it over?" he demanded.

"It's over," Jack said. "Stay out of my face, Bud Lowry!" he called as he walked to his truck.

The cops went back to the city building, laughing and shaking their heads.

62

Captain Billy taught me how to box. There was a homemade heavy bag hanging by a rope from a low branch of the big sapodilla, the dilly tree, in the backyard. Many summer evenings I remember, when the sun went down, that he would stand with his shoulder against the bag, giving me instructions as my small fists pounded away at the immovable, straw-stuffed canvas.

We would go to the weekly fights, too, where Billy would keep up a steady stream of advice on what each fighter was doing right, or more usually, wrong. He seemed to delight in going over to a corner when a fight ended, pumping some of that same advice he'd been giving me to the loser's trainer. Most of the trainers seemed to know Billy, and so he usually got away with it. Sometimes, however, they would tell him to get lost.

Carl never participated in these outings, and Billy never seemed to mind that his oldest son took no interest in standing in the backyard punching a bag hung from a tree. Phyllis's concern was that I not hurt my hands, and she didn't allow me to hit the bag bare-fisted.

Many nights Phyllis and Carl and I would be sitting in the Florida room at those times when Carl was ill, and Phyllis was reading to us while outside Billy was grunting and working out on the bag, his broad-muscled back slick with sweat under the spotlight that shone on the dilly tree.

Heart, Captain Billy always said. You're gonna be a good fighter, you've gotta have heart.

I didn't have the heart for it. Skill, technique, but no heart. I had a few fights in Golden Gloves while I was in high school. Billy was always in my corner, and every time I lost he'd say: "Son, your heart wasn't in it." Finally, I just quit boxing altogether.

There were nights occasionally when Captain Billy would come home late having been in a fight of his own. Too much to drink, an argument, and Billy was ready to scrap with anyone.

In my bedroom over the kitchen on William Street I'd sometimes be awakened when Billy came in from one of those fights. Phyllis would get up to tend to him. I'd hear them talking, Phyllis crying softly, asking why he had to do this while she cleaned a cut to his face. Eventually, she stopped getting up and Billy would take care of himself, grumbling, knocking things over as he stumbled around the kitchen.

It was amazing how much I had followed so undeterminedly in my father's footsteps, a man whose example I never set out to follow. Each time something happened now that brought me back to Captain Billy, I was alarmed by our similarities.

At the Cuban *grocería* I bought a bag of ice and carried it next door to the kitchen, where I put some of it in a towel, wrapping it around the back of my hand, which was already beginning to swell.

I called the Club manager and told him I was unable

to play tonight. He confirmed what Harry had said last night at the benefit. That unless business picked up, they were canceling our engagement for the rest of the summer. With a week's notice, of course. So after next week I'd be out a regular paycheck. I'd found Virginia Murphy's check this morning among the litter on the floor and put it back in the desk drawer.

Fucking Jack Bayard, I thought. Anyone else would have been happy to explain himself, to answer questions about something he clearly had an involvement in. But not Jack. No, Jack knew he couldn't be touched because who was going to say anything against the Bayards? Especially at this late date, assuming anyone who knew anything was still alive. Titus Walker was gone, Frank Paine. Virginia Murphy. All the principals. So Jack could afford to come unglued, slug it out in a public parking lot and threaten me with further retaliation if I kept going with this. As if this were all my doing.

As far as I was concerned, Jack had as much as confirmed his knowledge of what had happened to Lila Murphy by his reaction to my questions. Now all I had to do was find a way to prove it.

I picked up the phone and called Carl. His secretary said he was resting and had asked not to be disturbed. I told her to remind him that I was coming by at five. She said, yes, she had it on the appointment calendar.

The appointment calendar. That was our relationship. An appointment, just like anyone else who wanted to see the senator. I asked her to tell him that I was coming in the car, that I wanted to take him someplace, just so he would be expecting me. No surprises for the senator.

When I went back to the kitchen to refill the ice pack, Casey was at the door. "Bud, I came over as soon as I was able to get away."

"It's all right. Everything's under control."

"What did you do to your hand?"

"Hurt it."

She lifted the ice pack off and said, "Oh, Bud."

The flesh below my knuckles was turning blue, the skin all puffed up so tight I couldn't make a fist.

"Who did you hit?"

"Jack Bayard."

She didn't cry, but something in the way she looked at me reminded me of Phyllis. "Why?"

"He started it," I said. Feeling stupid when I realized how adolescent that sounded.

"God, is this ever going to end?"

I nodded. "I think so."

"What are you going to do?"

"Talk to my brother. He's dying. I want to make peace."

Standing beside my chair, Casey put her arm around my head, pulling my cheek against her stomach. "What's wrong with him?"

"Cancer." I felt her stomach muscles knot against my face.

"Jesus," Casey said. "Sometimes life sure sucks."

I couldn't have agreed more.

63

Carl wasn't wearing a tie. It was the first time in all his years of being in office that I could remember seeing him in public without a tie. He and Frank Paine had that in common. We walked out of his office, Carl limping toward the car. I held the passenger door of the Buick open for him. He backed into the car like a woman, sitting down and then bringing his legs inside. I closed the door and walked around the front of the car and got in behind the wheel.

"Where are we going, Bud?" Carl sat stiffly, his hands folded in his lap, staring straight ahead. Something about him reminded me of an old priest.

"It's a surprise. Something I want you to see."

As I reached down to turn on the ignition, he said, "What did you do to your hand?"

"I hit a guy."

"Aren't you a little old to start fighting again?"

"It was Jack Bayard," I said, glancing at Carl. "He came at me. I didn't have any choice." If Jack had said anything to him, Carl didn't register it now. He just shook his head disapprovingly. "How are you and Jack?" I asked.

"What do you mean, how are we?"

"I don't know. Your speech last night wasn't exactly Bayard politics."

"I thought we went over this once before. I don't know what you mean, Bayard politics."

"And why do I have a hard time believing that?"

"Because you've got something against the Bayards. I don't know what. But you're stubborn, Bud. You're just like Billy."

It was the first time I'd ever heard Carl mention our family in that way, connecting us to each other.

"Yes, I was thinking the same thing earlier," I said. "Except Billy was always on your side, the Bayard side. When they had one."

Carl looked out the window as we went over the bridge at Garrison Bight that divided the city marina, with the commercial fishing boats on one side, the pleasure craft on the other. Billy had kept the *Low Blow* down there. I wondered if Carl was thinking about that. At the light I turned left, heading south along the boulevard.

The sky was the color of lead, a blanket of clouds blotting out the sun.

"Remember when Phyllis used to read to us and Billy was outside punching the bag that hung from the dilly tree?" I asked.

We were going along the boulevard now, past the shopping centers and discount stores, all construction that wasn't here in those days.

Carl nodded, his face turned away, when it suddenly occurred to me that Carl had never been happy. What he wanted in life, he got, or at least what he always said he wanted. On the other hand maybe neither of us has been happy, making it a meaningless question. There is something about Carl, though, something that clings to him like the scar tissue around his damaged heart, that has kept us apart and deepened his mystery.

"Bud, I met with my attorney today," Carl said as we left Key West, crossing the bridge to Stock Island. "I'm making some changes to my will."

"I hope you're going to get a second opinion, maybe go up to New York. They've got more advanced cancer facilities up there."

"No better than Miami." Carl's tone suggested this was a closed issue. "Bud, where are you going?"

"It'll only take a couple of minutes."

Carl stared silently out the window for a while. "I'm leaving my house and office to the city," he said. "And I'm setting up a scholarship fund in my name."

Jesus. He wasn't leaving anything to chance, I thought. If he couldn't be sure of getting a bridge named after him, he would create his own memorial.

"What kind of a scholarship?"

"For any kid in the county who wants to pursue a career related to the environment."

The Carl Lowry Environmental Scholarship Fund. I couldn't help laughing.

"What's so funny?"

"It isn't funny. It's ironic." Actually it was pathetic, but saying so I would have risked being labeled cynical.

Carl shrugged as we rode past Bayard Cement and a couple of lumbering cement mixers turned onto the highway, belching diesel smoke and dripping gray water from their underbellies. *Buy Bayard by the Yard.* Carl had been buying it by the truckload for most of his life, and now as he approached the end, he was going to make amends with an environmental scholarship fund.

"I'm leaving you some money."

"Carl, I—"

"It isn't a lot but it will give you some security. I don't imagine there's much of that in the work you do."

It was said without contempt, but I understood that Carl would tolerate no further criticism implied or otherwise of his sudden political conversion. He made a production out of looking at his watch.

"It's almost five-thirty," he said.

"We'll be there soon. Don't worry, I'll have you back in time for your dinner engagement."

"Why can't you just tell me where we're going?"

I didn't say anything. We rode in silence. As we approached Bay Point and the Sugarloaf Lodge, I began to slow. Carl was fidgeting, picking at the crease in his trousers. Just before the Lodge I made a left onto a back road.

"What is this?" Carl asked.

Seconds later the bat tower loomed up ahead and I stopped twenty feet from its base and cut the engine. I turned and looked at Carl. A small tic was pulling at one corner of his mouth.

"Tell me about the Bayards," I said. "And Lila."

I got out of the car and walked over and looked up inside the bat tower at its empty interior. Carl refused to leave the car. Maybe I'd made a mistake bringing him out here. It had occurred to me after the angry encounter I'd seen Carl go through with Jack in the restaurant yesterday, and then his speech last night at the benefit, that Carl had broken with Jack Bayard in a way that no one would understand who hadn't watched their relationship from the very beginning, as I had.

I had no idea if Carl knew what had happened out here after Lila left the dance, but if he did—and if the split between him and the Bayards was real—then maybe, finally, he could deal with it. It was hard for me to think of him carrying this knowledge around all these years, but he was the last person left alive in Key West who could shed any light, I thought.

And Carl was dying.

A shitty thing to do, I thought, to use that as leverage, but I was doing it. My brother, who was leaving me money to provide for my financial stability.

I walked back to the car, leaning in his open window. "Carl."

"I want to go back to town." His voice sounded thin, almost desperate.

"I'll take you back, but first I want to tell you what I

think. My theory on what happened to Lila Murphy."

Carl looked straight out the windshield, his hands nervously plucking at his slacks.

"My theory is that one of the Bayards got Lila pregnant."

Carl's head went back against the headrest, and he closed his eyes.

"That was the reason there was no autopsy. Lila was pregnant, which in those days could be reason enough for murder. Lila was on the make. She was trying to land a big fish except she was relatively new here and she didn't know who she was dealing with when it came to the Bayards. How am I doing so far?"

I watched a stray tear escape one of Carl's closed eyes and run down his cheek. I didn't like this, but I had to do it. This was the only moment I was going to have with Carl. Once he got back to Key West, I knew he would be gone from me forever. Out of my control.

"The whole thing was hushed up," I continued. "In the way that only John T. could hush things around here in those days. He called in a few political debts. The chief of police. And the sheriff, Frank Paine."

I had to admit Frank was a question mark. From everything I'd learned about him he didn't seem to owe John T. political fealty. That bothered me. But I had convinced myself it didn't matter. Somehow the Bayards had gotten to Frank one way or another. It didn't change my theory.

"Lila left the dance. Jack was the point man for Peter. Or John T. He told her he had to talk to her and would meet her later. He'd pick her up, and established a time and place to meet. He stayed at the dance another half hour or so and then rendezvoused with Lila. They drove up here, and the rest, as they say, is history."

Carl's face was bloodless, his eyelids like dark

hollows. He stayed where he was, his mouth slack, and I watched his thin chest rise and fall in the shallow act of breathing.

"Except," I said, "except a couple of things. One, you were at that dance. You knew he was going out with Lila. You heard him set up the meeting with her later. Or maybe Jack confided in you. Which was it, Carl?"

I opened the door and put my hand on Carl's shoulder, nudging him, encouraging him to come out of it. He opened his eyes and looked into mine. It was a look of a man who has been betrayed, and I felt the weight of his eyes. We were brothers, after all. And these were our people.

"Those were the days when you were making your move. You were an aide to John T., but the following year you would be elected to the legislature. It was a heady time. Everything you'd dreamed of, and John T. was your patron. He made you, but he could also break you."

Carl swung his bad leg around and got out of the car. I helped him stand up. He took a couple of steps and staggered on the uneven, weed-grown ground. He looked off in the distance, staring at the sky, the bat tower, then started walking. He stopped about twenty yards away and knelt down on the ground, the way I had done, the way I had knelt here only a few weeks ago.

"Or maybe," I called, "it was the stranger. People remembered seeing a stranger talk to Lila. Maybe someone the Bayards hired."

Carl knelt with his back to me as if he were deaf to my words. I walked up behind him, knelt, and put my arm around him. "Your knowledge of this made you an accessory. You know that. But now your career's over. You've got nothing to lose. Put things right," I pleaded. "Do the right thing."

He turned his broken face to mine. "And what will you do?"

"Tell me it was Jack," I said, willing him to say it, to get this behind us. "I'll take him in and it will be over."

Carl shook his head and lowered himself closer to the ground. "Then you'd be bringing in the wrong man, Bud."

Carl's body trembled as though he were cold. I eased him back from the ground. "Carl, let me help you."

I led him, stumbling, over to the bat tower, where we sat leaning our backs against one of its leg supports. I had my arm around his shoulders, but he continued to tremble.

"Can you tell me about it?"

"What is there to tell? Except for the wrong man, you had it figured out."

"But why, Carl? Tell me why."

"Love?" He looked at me questioningly, as if I might not know the meaning of the word. Maybe I didn't.

"But she didn't love you, is that it?"

Carl shrugged. It was hard to imagine, cool, detached Carl venting his emotions over an unrequited love this way. Clearly, I did not know my brother.

"Was she pregnant?"

"Yes, she was."

"So your career would have been ruined."

He shook his head. "It wasn't my child."

Poor Carl. I viewed him now through the long lens of

time—a young man, inexperienced with women, drawn to a girl like Lila, feeling his first rejection, then shock and disillusionment when he learned that she was pregnant by another man.

"But you did go out with her. You had a relationship."

Carl laughed, a sound that was more like a bark. "Go out with her? Oh, yes, I went out with her. I was in love with Lila."

"So how did you know it wasn't your child?"

"Because she said it wasn't."

"And named someone else as the father?"

Carl nodded.

"One of the Bayards?"

Again he gave a simple nod of his head.

"Peter? Or John T.?"

"Peter."

Carl's best friend at the time. And recently married.

"So you were protecting him at the same time you were feeling Lila's rejection." Jesus. "But weren't there other solutions? Other ways around it? Did you have to kill her?"

Carl had his head in his hands. "I don't know what was in my mind that night, but I didn't plan it that way. I'd had a few drinks. We came out here, got into an argument. I pushed her. She fell and hit her head on something. I was scared to death. I ran and I left her here."

I watched white columns of smoke, probably from some nearby landfill, rise and flatten out against the leaden sky.

"Who knew about her?" I asked.

"What do you mean?"

"Who knew that you'd been with her?"

Carl shook his head, was silent a moment. Then he said, "Phyllis."

"You told her?"

He looked up at me and in a plaintive voice said, "Bud, she was the one anchor I had. I confided in her."

Phyllis.

And Frank Paine.

Yes, Phyllis had spent her life caring for Carl, protecting him, ensuring his physical well-being. She wouldn't let a youthful indiscretion get in the way and ruin everything she'd worked for. After all, Carl hadn't willfully done anything wrong. It was an accident.

"And the Bayards," I said.

"Peter and John T. knew."

"And John T. protected you because of Peter."

"We never talked about it."

There was a change in Carl. I'd first been aware of it last night, but it seemed absurd to believe that he had undergone some overnight conversion, had been transformed by the break with the Bayards, and that now the guilt he'd been carrying all these years was suddenly relieved by this confession, lifted like a weight from his soul.

Absurd but there it was. I was uncomfortable even thinking it. But Carl had stopped shaking. He looked out across the horizon toward Key West, and his blue eyes took on a lucidity I had never seen in them since he was a boy when his face burned with the rheumatic fever that nearly killed him. The irony of a rebirth now of course was that it had come just in time for Carl to die.

"How obligated to the Bayards were you? Was it because of Lila you maintained an allegiance to them?"

A half smiled played over Carl's lips. "Let me just say I feel like I've paid my debt to them."

"When did you come to that realization?"

He seemed to think about it. "The night you called and told me Virginia Murphy was in town."

Virginia.

There was, in spite of Carl's responsibility in that event, something depersonalized about Lila's death, rendered so perhaps by the lapse of time. I had no idea what I was going to do about it now. But Virginia was another matter. I knew her. I had spoken with her only weeks ago, only hours before she died. She was a client. There was nothing depersonalized about that.

"What do you know about Virginia's death?"

Carl shook his head. "Nothing."

I looked at him. He turned and stared back into my eyes. "I mean it. I really don't know anything."

I believed him. I had no reason not to believe him any longer. He had been sentenced already. "Do you think Jack—"

"Bud, I don't know."

"She called him. And he tried to return her call the night she died. What could have been the connection?"

Carl shook his head. "Lila. Lila. Jack had been hung up on her in high school. Virginia probably remembered him."

"He called her. Why? Did he know about Peter's involvement? Was he trying to protect him?" I knew it was probably the hardest question I could have asked Carl. Despite the apparent break in their political bond, they had a lifetime of a friendship between them.

Carl didn't hesitate. "I don't think so."

And again I believed him. In the silence that followed came the flat sound of a woodpecker tapping into the dead wood of a nearby tree limb.

66

Three navy jets screamed overhead, practicing touch-and-go exercises at the nearby navy base just off the highway on the ride home—dark silhouettes against the gray sky. In the gloomy light, the sea on either side of the highway was as gray as the road itself—a monotonous field of view that did nothing to elevate our moods. Neither Carl nor I spoke on the ride back into town, each of us absorbed with our own thoughts.

Fog, seldom seen in the Keys, hung over the city like a damp cape. When I stopped in front of Carl's place, I shut the motor off and waited. I knew what Carl's question would be before he asked it. I didn't know how to make it easy on him because I didn't have the answer.

The image of Kenneth Barlow standing in my hotel room in New Orleans came into my mind. A young man starting out in life who had made some mistakes and wanted advice. Perhaps I'd advised him wrong; perhaps if I'd stayed with him and brought him in, he would have been alive today. Or maybe I'd simply saved my own life. Life was filled with perhaps and maybe. In any case, Barlow was dead. Now a man at the end of his life wanted an answer, but all I could do was plead for time. Time to mull it over, think about it, put all the pieces together once more.

"What do you have to do?" Carl asked without looking at me.

"I don't know. I'll have to think about it. Will you be all right?"

Carl lifted his shoulders and brushed some soil from the sleeve of his shirt. "I trust you, Bud." Then he turned and offered me his hand. I shook it and Carl slowly got out of the car. When he closed the door, he turned back to me once more with that familiar thin smile on his face, then limped up the sidewalk to his office.

Virginia Murphy had trusted me. It was one of the last things I remember her saying.

I turned the radio on as I drove home and listened to an announcer reading the seven-o'clock news. Operation Cleansweep had been declared a mistrial today, just as Judge Watson predicted it would be. Without the testimony of Kenneth Barlow there had been insufficient evidence for the state attorney's office to proceed with the prosecution.

When I got home, I fed Tom, then sat down at the desk and let the night overtake me. I was surprised. In my depression I did not feel the desire to bury it in alcohol, a somewhat foreign sensation.

Later, in the dark, I fumbled for the phone and called Just. "You called it," I said when he answered.

"Only half of it."

"Now what?"

"I heard Farquar tendered his resignation almost as soon as he left court today, effective immediately."

"What prompted that?"

"Maybe a desire not to go to jail."

"Why would he have gone to jail?"

The judge chuckled. "He was caught in a bind. Seems George Lewis got a tip that the shoes of one of Farquar's defendants might match the imprint left in the ashes at your place. The guy was ready to testify that Farquar put him up to the break-in."

It was the only news I'd had today that could cause me to smile. George Lewis had come through for me.

Despite a few squeaks here and there, the wheels of justice still seemed to turn in the southernmost city in America. I hung up without saying anything about Carl. I did not feel right about seeking outside counsel on this issue, not even Just's. This was family, immediate family, and it was my call.

I spent the evening going from room to room, tinkering with the piano for a while in the bedroom, left hand only, while studying Lila's smile. I saw Carl as he'd been when he left the car earlier, his own smile as lopsided as his gait, the images of both of them blurring before my eyes.

My brother, Carl. As I struggled with the consequences of his act, I tried to separate myself from him, become a nonbrother, an acquaintance, something that only a few hours ago would have felt as natural as the keys beneath my fingers. But not now. Our relationship had changed in some imperceptible way, and it was impossible anymore to view him, his past, as distinct from mine.

I went out into the kitchen and made a sandwich, eating it standing up over the kitchen sink. Then I finished off the ice cream from the container I'd brought home for Casey and me the other night.

Afterward, I went back to the office and sat in the dark, looking through the venetian blinds, out the window and across the street to the glow of the Christmas-tree lights that hung year-round along the perimeter of the used-car lot, now dampened by the fog that still weighted the town on a night in June.

Could I turn Carl in? If I did, he would undoubtedly go to trial, a trial that could take months before it was placed on the docket. Months that Carl no longer had. Or had he paid his price, years of loneliness, defeated by the Bayards?

As defeated as I now felt.

The phone rang, stirring me from my tangled web. It was Casey.

"How did it go?" she asked.

"Oh, you know."

"Did you learn anything?"

"Hmmm."

"You okay?"

"Tired," I said. "A problem I've got to wrestle with."

"Want any help?"

"No, thanks."

She was silent a moment. "Call when you do," she said.

I hung up and went back to my refuge, the piano.

67

Other than to get in supplies I seldom left the house over the weekend. I settled in to reestablish order out of the chaos that was the result of several months' neglect, and the break-in the previous week. Each time Casey called, I put her off. Carl did not call, and though I thought about him constantly, I did not call him.

Portia Villani called Saturday morning. Her voice had lost some of its resonance, but she sounded in good spirits.

"Gideon, I spoke with your brother," she said. "And I want to tell you what I told him."

"Let me guess. You called about the speech."

"Yes, it was marvelous. I read it in the paper and

heard bits of it on the radio. It was the best benefit I can remember."

"Yes, I suppose it was."

"And thank you for your contribution."

"How are you feeling?"

"As well as someone my age can expect to feel. I'm now confined to a wheelchair."

"I'm sorry."

"But I am alive and after another week or so I hope you will come for a visit again."

"Of course."

"Phyllis would have been very proud. Of both you and Carl."

On Monday morning I had made my decision. I called Casey and asked if we could go to lunch. We agreed to meet at noon at the drugstore. Five minutes before noon I walked over and secured a corner table in the partitioned-off section away from the counter. Moments later the place was filled with the lunch-hour crowd of local-area businesspeople.

When Casey arrived, I stood and touched my lips to her cheek. After the waitress came and took our order, I told Casey about Farquar.

Her eyes misted over and for a moment I thought she was going to cry. Instead, she brushed some stray hair from her face, then smiled. "I can't believe I made such a serious error in judgment."

I shook my head. "This town's full of white-collar grifters, always has been. It wasn't your fault."

Casey reached across the table and put her hand over mine. "I'll make it up to you, Bud." She smiled.

The din back here with tables jammed close together was deafening. I leaned across the table and told Casey about Carl.

"Oh, Bud. What a nightmare this has been for you."

The waitress brought our iced teas.

"I want you to know that I haven't had a drink since the night I was arrested."

"You really don't have to tell me this."

"Yes, I do. Because I'm certain that I can beat this. But I'm equally certain I can do it without spilling my guts in front of a group of other drunks. I can do it on my own and with your help."

"I'm not putting any pressure on you, Bud. Each one of us has to make our own decisions. I will do what I can to help you. As long as you aren't drinking."

I nodded. "Fair enough."

"What are you going to do about Carl?"

"That's what I've been thinking about all weekend." I poured sugar in my tea. "I've decided to do nothing."

"Because of the cancer?"

"Partly. And I'm the only other person alive from either of the families involved. So what difference is it going to make to anyone?"

"What about Jack Bayard?"

"Under the circumstances, I don't think Jack is going to say anything."

"Have you talked to Carl?"

"Not since the other day. No."

Our food came and we ate, talking about different things: Casey's job, politics, the weather. When we finished eating, Casey went to the rest room and returned wearing a light glaze of fresh lipstick the color of a ripe mango. She sat back down.

"I've got something to tell you," she said.

"What's that?"

"I've been offered a job in Miami."

We looked at each other for a moment, and I smiled. "A good one?"

"Yes, better than anything I could do down here."

And that was the problem with Key West. For all of our sophistication we were still just a backwater at the end of the road with limited opportunities. A place people either came to drop out or renew themselves before heading back to the real world.

"Will you take it?"

"I haven't decided."

"Well, if you do, it's only a hundred and fifty miles up the road."

Casey nodded. We both knew, however, Miami was a world away for me, and part of the benefit of being there was the opportunity it offered Casey to meet people other than grifters and men marred by their past.

I paid the check and Casey and I walked out together. We hugged each other on the sidewalk, then parted.

I went home and called Carl. His secretary answered, saying that he was out and not expected in the rest of the afternoon. I told her who I was and gave her my number and asked her to leave a message for Carl to call when he came in, no matter how late.

I did not hear from him.

68

At nine the next morning I was drinking a cup of *café con leche* from the Cuban *grocería* next door and reading the paper when the phone rang. It was Carl's secretary: "You'd better come over."

I got on my bike and rode nine blocks across town to Carl's. A police car was parked out front and I heard the wail of an ambulance siren approaching. I dropped my bike and ran inside.

Carl's secretary sat at her desk with a look of shock frozen on her face. The door to the upstairs apartment was open and I climbed the stairs two at a time.

George Lewis was in the kitchen talking to a uniformed cop, who was relaying a message on a small two-way radio attached to the left shoulder epaulet of his uniform.

George glanced up at me when I came in. There were heavy pouches below his eyes and his skin looked yellow in the overhead fluorescent light that was on in the kitchen. "He's in the front room," George said. "It isn't pretty."

I walked down the hallway to the living room. Carl lay in the middle of the floor, the coffee table tipped over, his legs sprawled out at an odd angle. Blood and bits of flesh were spattered on the wall. The gun lay on the floor a couple of feet from his body. I recognized it as Captain Billy's pistol, the one he kept on the *Low Blow* for killing sharks, and that had now been used in the self-destruction of another member of my family. I couldn't remember Carl taking that pistol. Was it possible he'd somehow foreseen this happening when Billy died?

I sank to my knees beside him on the carpet and put my hand on Carl's chest. He was wearing a tie. I pressed my thumb and forefinger to my eyes and stayed there for several minutes. I heard the ambulance stop, the paramedics coming inside. I overheard one of them say,

"Shit, it's going to be tough getting him down on a stretcher with this turn in the staircase."

I put my arms under Carl and picked him up. He was so thin, so light. I walked down the hallway and stood at the top of the stairs. "I'm bringing him down," I said.

The funeral was Saturday. The lieutenant governor of Florida attended, along with several of Carl's colleagues from the Senate. Key West's funeral band played, marching behind the hearse that carried his body from the church to the cemetery. Sweetwater, I noticed, was in the band, playing the bass drum. I rode in a black limo provided by the mortuary that followed the band, with Casey, whom I'd asked to join me.

It seemed like half the town was in the cemetery. The day was bright, and hot, the orange flowers of a poinciana tree flaming brilliantly at one end of the cemetery while the flag above the Spanish-American dead drooped at half-mast in the breezeless air.

I saw Peter and his wife representing the Bayard family. I didn't see Jack. Peggy, of course, was there with her family, and Peggy wept openly. Webb and the courthouse crowd were there, along with George Lewis and Key West's police chief.

A color guard gave Carl a seven-gun salute, then presented me with the American flag that had draped his casket, folded in its customary triangle.

The media covered the story thoroughly, giving a detailed history of Carl's years as the representative for Monroe County, going back to that first election in the mid-fifties just before Captain Billy died. They made much of the fact that Carl, like his father before him, committed suicide rather than face a lengthy battle with the cancer that had afflicted them both.

I walked home with Casey and spent the rest of the afternoon sitting in my office.

That night Harry and I played the last gig of the summer at the Club. It was slow and melancholy, and about nine-thirty Casey came in and sat alone at the bar. I lifted my glass of club soda from the piano and silently toasted her.